As one of the thousands of children who marched with Dr. King, MARCH WITH ME has compellingly captured the essence of that historic and pivotal moment in time. I recommend MARCH WITH ME to avid readers everywhere. The publishing is especially timely 50 years later as the world remembers the contributions of young people of Birmingham (and everywhere) who helped "break the back" of segregation.

Carolyn Maull Mckinstry, marcher and Author *"While The World Watched"*

Reading Rosalie Turner's book "March With Me" reminded me of the profound struggles that both blacks and whites experienced in our efforts to desegregate our students and staff in the Bessemer City Schools. While serving as Assistant Superintendent and Superintendent during those years I spent many hours in the Federal Courts and in meetings with the school board and staff working out solutions that would benefit both races and maintain a viable school system.

Thanks to Rosalie for reminding us of the very personal struggles that both races were going through and showing us that struggles for the right things are seldom easy but never wrong.

I recommend that both students and adults read, "March With Me" to gain a perspective of the adjustments that they had to make during the 60s and how different that was from the life they are living today.

Larry O. Wilson, Superintendent of Bessemer City Schools (retired)

Hopefully one day none of us will have to say 'I'm sorry, I wasn't strong enough to stand up to any injustice perpetrated against another human being."

Thelma Ford Gibson, marcher in the Children's March

MARCH WITH ME

ROSALIE T. TURNER

CYPRESS CREEK PUBLISHING

Library of Congress Control Number:
ISBN 978-0-9792375-5-3

This is a work of fiction. Names, characters, places and events are
products of the author's imagination, while some of the people
and events are realistically depicted from the Civil Rights Era

Cover and text design by Darron Moore

Printed in the United States of America

First Edition

Cypress Creek Publishing
Florence, AL 35630

DEDICATION

This book is dedicated to all those who marched in
the Children's March
May 1963, Birmingham, Alabama—

(courage from the past)

and

to my five grandchildren:
Grace, Lexi, Kit, Abby, and Sophie Kate—

(hope for the future)

ACKNOWLEDGMENTS

I am grateful to so many for helping me with this book. The Birmingham Civil Rights Institute and the Birmingham Public Library were a tremendous help, with their excellent archives. The individuals who shared their stories and memories with me were Carolyn McKinstry, Thelma Ford Gibson, Pat and Willie Griggs, Kathy and Larry Manley, Alys and Larry Wilson, Jim and Serene Johnson, Donna and Ted Roose, Yvonne Willie and Elizabeth Rogers. Others who helped me in other ways were my editor Doann Houghton-Alico, Willie Cable, Dr. Fred Tarpley, and Carol Norton. Thanks also to my publicist, Stephanie Barko, and graphic designer, Darron Moore, and my publisher, David Messer.

AUTHOR'S FOREWORD

I had three main reasons for writing this book. First, I wanted to write about the Children's March. I consider it the first of several pivotal events that led our country to finally establish civil rights legislation. The other events, in my opinion, were the bombing of the Sixteenth Street Baptist Church resulting in the death of four children and the March on Washington in August of 1963. These are the events that caught the attention of the country and the government. The fact that most people in our country today have either forgotten or never knew about the Children's March was a strong motivation for my book.

The second reason for writing MARCH WITH ME came from meetings within the black community over the past few years. Conversation almost always came to the point of saying that young people today really have no understanding of what life was like before the civil rights movement and no realization of what that generation went through. Additionally, conversations in the white community expressed the same lack of real knowledge. Thus, I was determined to write a very readable account of what life was actually like for both blacks and whites during those turbulent years.

My third reason for writing this book, and probably my strongest, is based in my belief in the importance of reconciliation. I have seen across the entire country that, while people of different races are integrated, they still miss being connected on a deeper level. In order to make that connection a certain measure of reconciliation must occur. This can occur by the sharing of our stories.

My challenge to you, the reader, is to consider the questions at the end of the book and discuss them with friends and family, book clubs, community and church organizations, and other groups. My greater challenge is for you to get together with others of another race and have a dialogue to share ideas and understandings.

I thank you for reading MARCH WITH ME and hope it is meaningful for you.

Rosalie Turner
Birmingham, Alabama
January 10, 2013

March with me,
I'll march with you,
and so we will march together
as we march along.
Traditional camp song

Definition of a tornado - (and also, perhaps, the civil rights movement) - *a tempest distinguished by a rapid whirling and slow progressive movement*

PART ONE

The Civil Rights Years

PROLOGUE

April 1963
THE CIVIL RIGHTS MOVEMENT
BIRMINGHAM, ALABAMA

History weaves its silent strands around us, around and around us until we are part of its fabric. Later we wonder, "When did that happen? How did it happen?" History happens while we're living our lives: our everyday lives of going to school, going to work, going to the store, giving and taking, laughing and crying, dreaming and doing.

The strands of history wove their way into the flowering spring of that southern steel city, Birmingham, Alabama, in 1963, where two worlds existed: one for Negroes limited by invisible barriers, and one for whites, unaware that the barriers also limited them. It was a very different time, a time when whites and blacks lived completely separate lives, knowing nothing about the other's reality, much less their beliefs, hopes, and dreams. And so into the texture of life in Alabama were woven strands of mistrust, fear, and hatred: a perfect place for the civil rights movement to rip forth.

The civil rights movement hadn't really started with Rosa Parks, although she did get the nation's attention when she was simply so tired she didn't give up her seat on the bus in Montgomery, Alabama. But that had been eight years before. Eight years, and what had been accomplished since then? Sit-ins, beatings, attacks on the Freedom Riders, riots. Even Dr. Martin Luther King, Jr. had to admit there was not the hoped-for progress, especially after his failure to attract national attention and momentum for the Movement in Albany, Georgia, in the summer of 1962.

By April 1963, King and several other members of the Southern Christian Leadership Conference had developed a plan, and Birmingham was at the center. Wyatt Tee Walker, one of the founders of SCLC, thought a large nonviolent movement with direct action against the downtown businesses and government offices would provoke officials and law enforcement to such a strong reaction that the media would be attracted to their cause. King told them, "If we fill the jails with demonstrators, the focus of the country will be on Birmingham. How could the city leaders refuse to negotiate if that works?" But that didn't happen, and King began to despair.

Good Friday morning dawned overcast and humid. Indecision about what to do next filled the conference room. Should they march, knowing they would be arrested for parading without a permit? Possible bail money was drying up. Would it help or hinder the Movement to have the leaders and the few adult marchers in jail? Opinion shifted back and forth as tensions mounted. Finally, Dr. King and Rev. Abernathy appeared in their denim "work clothes." They would march. Rev. Shuttlesworth joined them for the first part of the walk which, of course, led to arrest and jail.

Eight days passed before Dr. King was released, yet even now, with King among them, Rev. Fred Shuttlesworth was still worried. Although he acknowledged that Dr. King's "Letter from Birmingham Jail" was getting some national attention, the Movement hadn't attracted the boost they had hoped for. *What was it gonna take?* he wondered as they met for a strategy session in Room 30 of the Gaston Motel not far from the Sixteenth Street Baptist Church in Birmingham. His fingers drummed the table, as his slim frame slouched in the chair. *I'm the one that encouraged Martin to come down here. I know how disappointing his push in Georgia was. He needs something big to happen. We haven't had a big success since Rosa Parks and the bus boycott in Montgomery. If he could make a change in Birmingham, why, that would make a huge difference what with Birmingham being the most racist place in America. We've gotten the media down here, but we're gonna lose them soon. We've got to do something!*

Rev. Shuttlesworth thought back to the mass meetings they had been having for several weeks, the meetings that were to stir the adults into marching with Dr. King. *Why wouldn't they march? Of course I know the answer, and I can't fault them. Lord, the atrocities we've seen and endured.*

"Martin," he began, "think about what life's been like for us here in Birmingham. How many times has the Klan bombed Bethel Baptist, my own church for heaven's sake, and my home when I've tried to desegregate things? Why do they call it 'Bombingham'—fifty unsolved bombings of our people in the last twenty years? Remember what the mob did to me when I took the children to desegregate Phillips High School? They almost killed me, man." He looked around the table. The men's stubbled faces and baggy, shadowed eyes were testimony to the ordeal they all felt.

Dr. King nodded solemnly. "I know. I know," he said. His fingers tapped against the white ceramic mug that held cold, bitter coffee.

"And what happened at the meeting with our folk last night, let me ask you that? We're not gonna get the adults, Martin, and that's a fact. They're too frightened."

They both sat silently, remembering the emotional meeting with a group of adults the previous evening.

"Dr. King," one man stood, dressed in a worn but well-ironed blue shirt and khaki pants, "We understand what y'all wanna do here, but look at it for us. You come and get things all stirred up, then y'all go away, and we're left with the mess; no jobs, the Klan after any a' us that marched. What you think's gonna happen to us then?" He sat down, a frown on his dark, lined face.

"I do understand, but y'all need to look at the big picture, what marching will accomplish," Dr. King responded.

A woman jumped up and shook her finger at Dr. King. "The big picture? Let me tell you something. The 'big picture' is what we made for our ownselves here. We keep our children safe, Dr. King. We keep our neighborhoods close-knit so we watch over everybody's children. Our churches, our schools, our neighborhoods—they be the center of our lives. We built up our own businesses on Fourth Avenue so our children don't need never to go downtown and find out the hard way how the whites treat us. We look out for all the children as long as we can. And we, grown-ups, we walk the straight line so we don't agitate no whites. We do our work, we never look them in the eye, we never 'spect them to call us Miz or Mister, and we stay quiet. We know what we got to do to survive." Her voice rose even louder, her hands punctuating every word. "And y'all come here, stirring trouble, causing riots, and who's gonna get hurt? Us. We lose our jobs, or our houses, or even our lives, Dr. King. And that's the 'big picture.'" She sat down to a chorus of amens and "tell it, Sister."

Dr. King held up a conciliatory hand. "Sisters and Brothers, I know what you go through down here. We walk the same path. But we have to end it. We have to get the nation to pay attention, to get Washington to pay attention, so we can have legislation that will change things. Keeping your children close and safe is good, but they are not free. It's freedom we need to experience life fully, to be all we can be, to have the jobs we deserve."

Dr. King had shared all the reasons for marching: how by filling the jail the world would see how bad things were in the South, and legislation would be enacted to bring about change; how the black schools didn't have nearly the resources of the white schools; how black teachers were paid only 60 percent of what white teachers made; how the job market could open up with integration; how limited the world was for blacks in the South. But it didn't matter. The adults wanted no part of marching, and that evening's meeting convinced the leaders.

The new man in the group, Rev. James Bevel, broke the lengthening silence and spoke up. "You called me here, Martin; now why won't you listen to my plan?" His piercing, dark eyes held Dr. King's gaze for a moment, as if the fire in them could sear through Dr. King's reluctance.

Dr. King shook his head. "I'm listening, James, but I can't go along with you. Certainly we can use the help of the students from Miles College to march with us, but not the younger children. It could be dangerous."

"Dangerous?" exclaimed Rev. Abernathy. "Of course, it's dangerous, Martin. It's dangerous for all of us every day."

"That's no reason to expose children to the risk."

Bevel leaned forward with intensity. "You want to fill the jails, don't you? I can guarantee hundreds, thousands of kids. You want to get TV coverage, don't you? I can't think of a better way. This'll work, Martin. I'm sure of it."

Rev. Shuttlesworth thought about Bull Connor, the Commissioner of Public Safety, whose hatred against blacks was legendary. *Would he take action against children?* Rev. Shuttlesworth couldn't answer that. *But now is the time. I've been working since the '50s, and are we any better off today? No. We've got Martin here. We've got the media coverage. Let's move with it. Sure, I was hesitant to bring in Bevel with his reputation as a hothead, but he was doing a great job in Mississippi getting voter registration. He does get results. We're all members of SCLC, and we're all working for the same thing.*

Rev. Shuttlesworth put his hand on Dr. King's arm. "Let's listen to what James has to say. You've been calling this 'Project C' for confrontation. Now is the time for that confrontation, Martin."

Rev. Bevel acknowledged Shuttlesworth's support with a

nod. "Look at who's the most responsive at our evening meetings. These kids are fired up." Bevel continued, "They're ready, and we need them."

Dr. King nodded reluctantly. His thoughts turned to the children, how naïve they were, how they loved the idea of keeping their possibly marching a secret from the grown-up world. At the last mass meeting when he'd called for those who were willing to march with him to stand up, it was the young people who had stood. They would march, he knew, but any resulting violence would shatter their innocence once and forever. Could he allow that?

The next few days and nights were even more intense as Dr. King anguished and prayed. Rev. James Bevel preached to and coaxed the young people. Shelley "the Playboy" Stewart and "Tall Paul" Dudley White, popular black DJs on radio station WENN, urged the kids on with coded words.

Negro kids knew that when Shelley Stewart gave his jive talk about having a party or a picnic, he was really talking about marching for the Movement. They had come to identify certain songs with what they were going to do, and all this time parents and other adults were kept in the dark about the hidden meanings. School and athletic student leaders slipped away to lunch meetings at the Gaston Motel with Rev. Bevel to learn how to secretly spread the word. Little cards that could be hidden from adults were passed out saying "Fight for freedom. Then go to school." Their parents knew the DJs had started talking to the young people about the injustices in their world, but they had other things on their minds, and so they missed the warning flags of what was to come.

Tensions, excitement, determination, and fear grew as the warp and weft wove together forming the final tapestry.

Finally, there were the children. And history happened.

CHAPTER ONE

Tornado: *A violent, whirling wind; a tempest distinguished by a rapid whirling and slow progressive motion.*

April 1963
LETITIA

"Letitia! Run!" Mae yells.

"I can't see! The rain," I shout back, trying to wipe the water away from my eyes. The sky's getting darker and darker.

I hear the wind moaning through the trees, feel it whipping my skirt against me, and my heart beats faster. We're still blocks from our homes. I hold my schoolbooks tighter as I run, my breathing in gasps as the rain pelts me.

"In here!" Mae darts toward the entrance of a café.

I hesitate, even though the rain is stinging.

"It's OK. It's not the white one."

Now I see where we are, and know that Negroes can go in the front door of this place. Two steps closer and a bicyclist zips up beside me.

"Lettie," my older brother, Sam, yells. "Get on the handlebars. Quick!"

I glance at Mae, and Sam yells again, "Hurry!" Mae waves good-bye, and she ducks into the café. I dump my books in the bike's basket and try to climb on. Sam hasn't ridden me on his handlebars since I was a kid. I'm petite like Mama Lucy, my grandmother, but I don't think this will work.

"No! Get on the bar." He jerks me on in front of him.

I grab the handlebars too, and he takes off, peddling like anything. Spray of wind and rain slaps my face. Sam stands to get more power, and I hold on tighter.

"I'm going to fall off!"

"No, you're not. Hang on." I can hardly hear his voice above the wind.

We fly the few blocks, and he slides into our driveway. The sky is full dark by now, the roar of wind all around us. I grab my books before his bike hits the ground, and we race to the back door. Mama and Etta, our five-year-old sister, are standing there with the door open. Mama's arms are reaching to pull us into the room.

"Thank you, Jesus!" she exclaims.

My ponytail drips cold water down my neck. Etta's holding out some towels for us, and as we dry off, she asks, "Were y'all scared?"

Sam and I exchange glances. "Nah," says Sam.

I admit, "I was kinda."

Mama's watching out the window. I know if she thinks we're in that tornado's path, she'll squeeze us into the hall closet. I go to her side and look out. The tree in our backyard is weaving crazily, and some neighbor's laundry blows across the yard. The sky, though, doesn't seem quite as dark.

Seconds tick by into minutes. Finally, I hear Mama let her breath out as if she's been holding it all that time. She turns back to the kitchen, and I know the danger has passed.

"What a day for my birthday," I complain as I gather the towels to spread them out.

"Now, don't you fret none, sugar," Mama Lucy says as she comes into the kitchen from her little room at the back. "You'll have a good birthday no matter the weather." She grabs hold of the table edge and slips weakly into a chair.

"I'm fixin' your favorite supper too," Mama adds.

Etta gives me a hug. "And I'll sing you 'Happy Birthday.'" I hug her back.

"Ain't ya gonna thank me for saving you?" Sam asks, his teasing smile lighting up his face.

"Don't say 'ain't,' and I coulda gone into the café with Mae and been safe."

"But I braved the wind and rain to get you."

"'Cause Mama made you," pipes up Etta, and we all laugh. I start up to the room I share with Etta. Sam can't resist one more dig. "Did Marcus tell you 'happy birthday'?" I glare at him. How he ever figured out I like Marcus, I'll never know.

I hear Etta ask "who's Marcus?" as I scoot up the stairs. I want to write in my diary before Etta comes up. She's getting so nosy about everything I do. I pull the little pink book from under my slips in the top drawer and take the key from under my corner of the mattress.

Sitting cross-legged and leaning on the headboard of the bed I start to write.

Dear Diary,

Today is my fifteenth birthday. The best thing that happened today is that Marcus told me 'happy birthday.' Of course, Mae had to tell him it was my birthday, even though I'd mentioned it last week. Still, he smiled when he said it.

I sit back and remember.

There'll be a singing at church next weekend. Maybe I'll get to sit next to him. Maybe he'll even ask to walk me home. Maybe . . .

"Watcha doin'?" blurts Etta as she bursts into the room.

"Can't you ever just walk in quietly?" I snap. She looks at me with such a crestfallen expression that I make my voice gentler. "It's only 'cause I like to be alone sometimes."

"Why?"

"You'll understand when you're older."

"You always say that." She climbs on the bed and puts her head in my lap. I close and lock my diary. "Lettie, what d'ya wanna be when you grow up?"

I know she's my sister, but why does she have to be such a pain? She cuddles closer. I imagine Mama whispering in my ear to be nicer to her 'cause she's still little. Darn! I take a deep breath, trying to stop from telling her to scram. That never does any good anyway.

"You know I wanna be a teacher." I give up on having some private time. I stroke her face, the same chocolate shade as Daddy's. I'm more what Mama calls caramel like Mama is, and so is Sam.

Etta's black-button eyes look up at me from her round little face. "Why you wanna be a teacher?"

"I've told you a hundred times."

"Tell me again."

I sigh. "There's not many choices for colored girls. I sure don't wanna be a maid like Mama is to that Miz Pierce over the mountain. By being a teacher I can help colored kids get an education."

"Is it bad to be a maid?"

"'Course not. Mama works hard at what she does. I don't want to be bossed by any white lady is all."

Etta's eyes flutter closed. I sit quietly with her head in my lap and let my thoughts drift to plans for this weekend. We stay like that until Sam yells that supper's ready.

It's like we all have assigned seats around the kitchen table. Mama and Daddy, then Etta and Mama Lucy are on one side, and Sam and I are on the other.

Daddy's washing his hands at the sink as Mama puts the bowls of greens and mashed potatoes on the table. The thick slices of ham are already there. I see that Mama put the plate of cornbread right in front of my place, and I smile.

When Daddy sits down he looks at me and winks. "Happy Birthday, Lettie."

"Thanks, Daddy."

He says his usual grace. Dishes and silver clank against the Formica tabletop, and everyone starts talking at once. It's always like this. Usually, once we start eating it gets quieter, until Sam starts talking. He always gets us laughing about something.

"Did you get caught near that tornado, Daddy?" Etta asks.

"No, thank you, Jesus. I was pretty worried about y'all, though."

Sam puffs out his chest. "You didn't need to worry none. I went on my bike and rescued Lettie. All I needed was my Superman cape."

Etta shakes her head. "You don't got a Superman cape."

"Well, I should have since I was faster than a speeding bullet as I raced Lettie home to safety."

We all groan at his silliness.

When Mama brings in my birthday cake—my favorite, chocolate cake with vanilla icing—they all sing "Happy Birthday" to me. I count the candles, fifteen and one to grow on, then make my wish. Everyone claps as I blow them all out in one breath.

"I bet I know what your wish was," Sam can't resist saying. "Somethin' about Marcus." He laughs as I jab my elbow into his side.

"Don't be teasing your sister," Mama says, but telling Sam not to tease is like telling him not to breathe.

"Letitia," Daddy's voice is serious. "For your birthday we put some more money in your college fund. Won't be long till you're going to be needing it."

"Thank you, Daddy." The gift is no surprise. It's what they've been doing every birthday since I was five.

"No cake for me," Mama Lucy says as I pass her a plate. "This sugar has me feelin' poorly lately. Doctor tell me don't eat no more sweets."

Daddy sits back as Mama and I start to clear the table. "They's talk at the mill that Rev. Shuttlesworth is getting Dr. King to come to Birmingham."

Sam sits up straighter. "Dr. King? Here in Birmingham?"

"That's right. Say they's going to be meetings at our churches to talk to us about protesting."

TURNER

Sam and I glance at each other. We've heard the talk too. When Sam isn't giving out his jive talk, he and I have long talks about Dr. King. I know Sam wants to be part of anything Dr. King might bring to Birmingham.

"Well," Mama says, "Rev. Shuttlesworth has tried to get the civil rights movement going here for years and nothing's happened. I doubt if Dr. King can make a difference."

Daddy shrugs and lights up a cigarette. Mama Lucy gets up in her shaky way. "Letitia, honey, come into my room for a minute. I got something special for you."

I follow her into the tiny room Daddy fixed for her out of what used to be our back porch. I can't imagine what she has for me. She picks up a small package from the table and sits on her bed, patting a place next to her.

"Sugar, of all my grans, you is the one that's got my spirit. I had to have lots of grit an' courage to get through everything to where I am today. You got the same inside you. Use it for the right things, Letitia, honey. For the right things, hear?"

I'm not sure I understand her words, but they touch me. I slowly unwrap the package she hands me. Inside is a gold locket I've seen her wear from time to time.

"Mama Lucy, it's beautiful. Thank you." I kiss her leathery cheek.

"I had Sam help me fix it up. Look inside."

I open the tiny catch and inside the locket is a picture of Mama Lucy. "How did you do this?" I ask in astonishment. I've never seen a picture of my grandmother except for the wedding picture she keeps on her bureau.

She chuckles. "That Sam. He can do anything he sets his mind to. He done borrowed a camera from the church."

"This is wonderful. The best present I ever got." I almost want to cry.

"They's a reason, sugar, I want you to have this. All your life, I been telling you about those who came 'fore us, your ancestors. I told you about all their struggles, about how strong they

12

had to be to survive."

I nod.

"You need to be 'membering them. You got their blood in your veins. A time is coming, sugar, a time is coming when you'll need that same strength inside you."

"You mean if Dr. King comes here?"

She puts her small, gnarled hand over mine. "You'll know when. And I'm hoping that when you look at my picture, you'll 'member, and you'll find that strength."

CHAPTER TWO

All happy families resemble one another; every unhappy family is unhappy in its own fashion.
    Leo Tolstoy, *Anna Karenina*

April 1963
MARTHA ANN

Martha Ann shifted around in bed pulling the pillow over her head, but she couldn't block out the sounds. She knew the pattern that would follow: her father's voice raised in angry shouts; her mother's pleading, then weeping; the sound of doors slamming; her father's car starting up, then the squeal of tires against the driveway. The silence that came next was almost as disturbing. Should she go to her mother? Should she stay awake and make sure her father comes home safely? She never knew.

Her bedroom door squeaked open, and Brad's head was silhouetted by the hall light.

"Are you awake?" he whispered.

Martha Ann sat up in bed and opened her arms wide for her younger brother.

When he climbed in beside her and leaned into her warmth, his tears felt cold against her arm.

"It's OK now," she said. "It's over."

"But why does Daddy have to yell like that? Why's he so mad at Mommy?"

Martha Ann shook her head. "I don't know. He didn't used to be that way."

"Poor Mommy," said Brad.

Poor us, thought Martha Ann, as the two snuggled down and eventually drifted asleep.

The next morning spilled sunshine over the Pierce's house as Martha Ann got ready for school. When she came into the kitchen, her father was setting down his coffee cup. He grabbed the car keys and headed out the door. "I'll see y'all tonight."

"Have a good day, dear," said Mrs. Pierce, a bright smile on her face.

Martha Ann looked from one parent to the other and began to wonder if she had dreamt the whole thing the night before. One glance at Brad's confused expression assured her it had not been a dream.

"Bye, Daddy," they both said.

"I'll drive y'all to school as soon as you're ready." Mrs. Pierce, dressed in her favorite yellow shirtwaist dress and heels, cleared her husband's breakfast dishes from the table. "I need to get home quickly 'cause this is one of Willa's days to help me."

"Mom," began Martha Ann, "last night—"

"Now, don't you worry about last night, darlin'. It was nothing. Nothing." She turned back toward them, the smile on her face not reaching into her eyes. "Finish up. I need to be going."

The hubbub of noise as Martha Ann entered Shades Valley High School provided a comfortable blanket of familiarity. Seeing Molly and Connie in the throng ahead of her helped push away the shadowy remnant of her parents' fight.

"Are you ready for the biology test?" Martha Ann asked Molly as she caught up to her friends. No point asking Connie. She was the top student and always ready for any test.

"I'm kinda worried about it," admitted Molly.

They entered their homeroom, and Martha Ann walked to her desk, plopping her books down.

"Were you scared yesterday?" a voice startled her from behind.

She turned. "Oh, Tommy. Yesterday? What do you mean?" *He can't know about my parents, can he?*

"I was afraid we were gonna have a tornado. It got so dark out."

"A tornado? I guess I wasn't thinking about that. No, I wasn't scared. I was home already when the storm got so bad."

"OK," Tommy said as he ambled back to his seat.

Gosh, did I sound stupid? I should have asked him something, kept talking. Why is it so hard to know what to do with boys? I wish I was more like Sandra. Darn!

Martha Ann's gaze went to the attractive blonde standing in a circle of boys by the window. They were all laughing at something she had said. *Sandra makes it look so easy. When will I be like that?*

Martha Ann moved through the day, her thoughts filled with schoolwork, her friends, plans for the weekend. It wasn't until after school, back in her bedroom, that the unease slipped in again. She changed from her school clothes to a pair of shorts and a white cotton blouse and sat cross-legged on her bed with her diary in her lap.

DearDiary,

I want to tell Connie and Molly about last night, but I really don't want them to know what's going on between Mom and Daddy. It scares me. I don't know why Daddy is like that now. Maybe he might get so mad he'd hit Mom. Maybe they're going to get a divorce. I'd be so embarrassed if they did. I'd be the only one in my class whose parents are divorced. Why can't things be like they used to be?

With the light knock on her door Martha Ann stuffed her diary under her pillow. "Come in," she called.

"Here's your clothes I ironed, Miss Martha Ann," said Willa, bringing in an armload of dresses, skirts, and blouses on hangers and putting them away neatly in the closet.

"Thanks, Willa." Martha Ann got up and slipped downstairs to see if anything interesting was on the television.

"So, how was school today?" after a few bites of meatloaf her father asked his usual question, as the family sat at the supper table. This return to ritual made Martha Ann begin to relax.

"Fine," she answered.

"There was a fight at school today," Brad jumped in with enthusiasm. "It was Jim and Walt. They had to go to the principal's office."

"Why were they fighting?" asked Mrs. Pierce.

Brad shrugged. "I dunno. Something Jim said made Walt mad."

"They shouldn't be fighting at school," began Mrs. Pierce.

"That's boys. Boys will be boys. Don't make a big thing out of it." Mr. Pierce scowled at his wife, and her shoulders sagged. She looked down at her plate. The tension hovered in the air, almost tangible, for a moment.

Mrs. Pierce straightened up and smiled at Martha Ann. "How was that test you had? Biology, wasn't it?"

"Yes, ma'am," Martha Ann answered, glad for a safe topic. "It wasn't too bad. I think I did OK."

"Well, good for you. I liked biology when I was in high school. I thought the labs were fun."

"I like it too. Poor Molly, though. She hates it. She doesn't like cutting up worms and stuff."

"You get to cut up worms?" Brad's eyes lit up.

Everyone chuckled, and Martha Ann thought even the house breathed a sigh of relief as though things were normal again.

"Well, I'm glad you're on the college track, Martha Ann. It's so important that girls get a college education today." Mrs. Pierce nodded strongly, emphasizing her point.

"What about boys?"

Mrs. Pierce smiled at Brad. "It's always been important for boys. Girls didn't used to be pushed to go to college, but it's just as important for them to get a good education."

"Well, I'm going to the University of Alabama," announced Brad, "and I'm gonna play football for them like Joe Namath."

Mr. Pierce clapped him on the back. "That's my boy!"

Martha Ann liked to do her homework on the kitchen table. There was something comforting about the sounds of family around her—her dad watching TV in the living room, Brad stretched at his feet with toys, her mom cleaning up from dinner. *Anyone looking at us through the window would think we're a nice, regular family. Sometimes, like now, I can even pretend that we are, but then it never lasts. She shrugged away the thoughts and continued her homework.*

She paused with her pencil in her hand. "Mom, why is it so important for me to go to college? I don't have any idea what I want to be, to do with my life."

"That's OK, sugar. You have lots of time to decide. The important thing is to get that college education so you can get a job and support yourself."

"Mom! Don't you think I'll get married?"

Mrs. Pierce smiled and came over to give Martha Ann a hug. "'Course I do. Any man would be lucky to have you for a wife. It's only that . . ."—her smile slipped away—"it's that you never know what will happen in life and you need to be prepared." She grabbed up the dishrag and wiped the counter. "Look at me. If anything happened to your father, why, I have no skills, no way to earn a living."

"Mom—" Martha Ann felt a cold knot of fear in her stomach.

Mrs. Pierce stopped wiping and looked at Martha Ann. "But we don't have to worry about that. Your father's got a good job and everything's fine." She turned back to her work. "Everything's fine."

~

The night crept slowly over them. Martha Ann listened closely as she got into her pajamas, brushed her teeth, and gave her hair the hundred strokes she'd read about in Seventeen. She could hear an occasional comment from her dad or mom over the droning of the TV. She climbed into bed and turned off the lamp. She tried to relax into sleep, but her ears strained for any sounds of anger. Little by little, though, her shoulders relaxed, her breathing became slow and deep, and sleep carried her away.

CHAPTER THREE

There is scarcely a consequential interaction between a black and a white in the United States in which race is not a factor. . . . It may provoke aversion, fear, or just awkwardness.
David K. Shipler, *A Country of Strangers: Blacks and Whites in America*

April 1963
LETITIA

We hurry through dinner to get to the mass meeting. It'll be hard to get a seat with Dr. King speaking. Clearing the dishes after dinner, I think about the excitement of hearing Dr. King and maybe sitting by Marcus too. Why does Mama pick this time to tell me I'm gonna have to help next Saturday with the birthday party for Miz Pierce's daughter?

"Mama, I don't wanna go. I don't wanna be anywhere near that white girl's sweet sixteen party." My shoulders sag as we head to the car.

Mama gets that look, and I know I don't have a chance. "I need your help doing the cleanup," she says. "We'll catch the bus at 11:30 Saturday, and that's all there is to it."

I sigh big and climb into the car. Mama's been working for Miz Pierce two days a week for a few years now, but I've never had to go. *How can I become invisible?*

When we get to St. John's A.M.E. Church, I see Mae and her family across the aisle. We wave to each other. I was hoping all the kids would get to sit together, but I can see we won't be able to. I lean around Sam and spot Marcus, Tyrone, and Damon

in the back pew. I smile at them, and Sam elbows my side.
"Bet you wish you could be sitting back there," he whispers
to me as we settle in a pew toward the front. I give him a dirty
look. He laughs quietly. The organ plays in the background.
"Brothers and Sisters, welcome," begins Rev. Thomas. "Let
us put our minds on Jesus as we open with prayer." His voice rolls
out from deep in his chest and carries us along to some higher
place. The choir sings "Swing Low, Sweet Chariot" and we sway to
the rhythm. We pray and we sing, our arms rising up to the Lord.
"Amen." "Hallelujah." "Um hmm." "Yes, Lord." Now we're ready
for Dr. King when he arrives. Just knowing he'll be here makes
a hum of electricity run through the whole congregation. Every
pew is full, and people are standing along the walls. We all keep
glancing to the back, just waiting for him to come through those
doors.

Then, finally, it's like a spark goes off. And everyone's head
swivels around as Dr. King, Rev. Shuttlesworth, and Rev. Abernathy sweep into the sanctuary and make their way to the front.
We're all on our feet, clapping and smiling. Those on the ends of
the pews reach out toward Dr. King, just to touch the great man
himself. He nods this way and that, but his expression is very
serious. Rev. Shuttlesworth and Rev. Abernathy are smiling and
saying hello to people as they come down the aisle, but not Dr.
King.

Rev. Thomas steps forward and shakes hands with our
three famous guests, then gestures for Dr. King to take the pulpit,
but Dr. King motions for Rev. Abernathy to go first. As Rev.
Abernathy stands behind the pulpit and looks over the crowd, the
three other ministers take seats behind him.

"We're on the threshold of freedom here in Birmingham,
Alabama," he tells us. "If the Negro is to be free, he must free
himself." Sam nods, as if Rev. Abernathy was talking right to
him. As the reverend preaches on to us, people in the congregation say "Yeah" with voices sometimes angry. Even so, sometimes
he makes us laugh. When he finishes, we all stand and clap. He

smiles and waves, then steps back. Dr. King comes to the pulpit. We applaud even louder. This is what we've been waiting for.

But Dr. King can't start speaking 'cause we're still standing and clapping. He keeps raising his hand for us to stop, and, finally, we do. We sit, and silence fills the church.

When he starts speaking, Sam leans forward, like he's got to take in every word. Dr. King's voice vibrates around us, pulling us together, pulling us close to him. "There are those who write history. There are those who make history. There are those who experience history. I don't know how many historians we have in Birmingham tonight. I don't know how many of you could write a history book, but you are certainly making history and experiencing history. You will make it possible for the historians of the future to write a marvelous history."

The power of his voice goes on and on. He talks to us about the injustices that have always been part of our lives here. I feel the tension in Sam's arm as it brushes my own. I look down and see his clenched fist. Dr. King talks about the importance of nonviolence. He talks about love, different kinds of love, and his words make sense to me. I believe him when he says love can make the difference of going the second mile to restore a broken community.

"We will have a new Birmingham, and you will transform these very people who have stood up against us all these years. This is the meaning of love and the meaning of nonviolence. We will be able to make this a new and great city." Sam is one of the first on his feet, clapping and cheering those words, but I am right beside him, doing the same, and so is everyone in the sanctuary. The noise bounces around the room carrying such power. Sam glances at me. His smile and shining eyes tell me that he believes in the Movement, and he can see that now I do too.

It takes a long time for all of us to settle down. We know Dr. King has to speak at several churches tonight, but we don't want to let him go so we keep on applauding. Finally, he, Rev. Shuttlesworth, and Rev. Abernathy head down the aisle and out the door. We settle back into the pews, sighing like we've just run a big race or something. Rev. Thomas closes with a prayer, and, suddenly it seems, the evening is over.

Driving home, Daddy says, "He a wonderful speaker, still, I don't believe he gonna get many to march with him." I feel Sam's excitement as he sits beside me. He's gonna march, I know.

Mama nods her head. "I don't know nobody who's gonna march. Miz Pierce did tell me last week that all the white ladies over the mountain gonna fire their maids if they do the marching with Dr. King. Law, I can't imagine those ladies getting a thing done without their maids."

Daddy chuckles.

"But, truth to tell," Mama adds, "Miz Pierce didn't call him Dr. King. She say 'that colored man who come down here causing trouble.' Humph." Mama is a tall, slim lady, but when she's mad she draws herself up and looks even taller. All my friends think of her as quiet and sweet, and she is, but at home she's like that sturdy oak tree out back. You don't want to mess with Mama 'cause there's no give in her.

Saturday comes too soon for me. The air has that clean, fresh smell of spring, but I can't enjoy it as I trudge with Mama to the bus stop. She's wearing her black dress and carrying a neatly pressed white apron, not really a uniform since she doesn't have to wear one, but it's what Miz Pierce told her to wear. I'm in a white blouse and my old, gray skirt. When the bus belches to a stop, Mama goes up the front steps and pays our fare then gets off, and we move to the back entrance and climb aboard. I'm glad we can find seats in the back and don't have to stand.

The bus lumbers up and over Red Mountain. I sit with my head down, making sure Mama knows how much I hate doing this.

Mama's voice is quiet but firm. "Letitia, I know you don't want to go with me, but I need your help or I'd be there till late tonight cleaning up. You'll be in the kitchen washing dishes. You won't be having to serve no white kids, so don't you be worrying about that."

I glance over at her. Mama pats my hand, and I give her a little smile.

Once we get off the bus we still have to walk a few blocks to their house. The yards are so much bigger than in our neighborhood, so many trees and bushes, and flowers blooming in neat flowerbeds, and lawns that look like green carpets. I notice that it's quieter here, no neighbors sitting on the front porch calling out to people as they pass.

"Here we are," announces Mama. I glance at the brick house. It sits back from the street, and we walk around to the back door. My feet get heavier and heavier and my steps slower. Mama looks back at me and scowls, so I hurry and catch up.

Miz Pierce herself opens the door. She's a little shorter than Mama and much rounder. The cream-colored dress she's wearing looks a size too small and makes her pale skin look even more washed out. Her dark hair is poofed high like she's just come from the beauty parlor.

"Thank goodness you're here, Willa," she exclaims after Mama introduces me. "You need to get going on those sandwiches."

Mama and I spend the next hour cutting the crusts off the bread (the best part, I think) and making dozens of little sandwiches: chicken salad, pimento cheese, and a weird one with cream cheese and cucumber. The next hour is spent setting out everything on a huge table covered with a white lace cloth in the dining room. We set out plates with a pretty rosebud design, the punch bowl—a huge glass thing—with cups, and silverware that Mama said she polished all one day last week. I guess this girl's whole class is coming to her party.

I peek at the living room. There's a sofa and matching chairs in a gold color, and lemon-colored sheer curtains hang from the top of the big windows to the floor. The room is about as big as our whole downstairs. Well, maybe it's not quite that big.

We're in the kitchen filling all these platters with fancy

cookies when the girl comes in. She glances at us and says, "Hey, Willa. Where's my mom?" Her sandy brown hair is in the popular way for whites, straight and curving at the chin line. I know the style 'cause it's in all the magazines. She runs her hand through her hair and kinda flips it back like whites do.

Mama nods at her. "Hello, Miss Martha Ann. Your mama's in the dining room. This here's my daughter, Letitia."

She looks at me for the first time. "Hey," she says as she quickly turns. She's not as tall as her mama, but she's slim. Her dress is sailor-style, a white top with a big collar trimmed in the same navy blue as the skirt. As she leaves the room she calls, "Mom, I need you to pin on my corsage."

I look at Mama, and she looks at me. "Corsage?" I mouth the word, wearing the same expression I have when Mama fixes brussels sprouts for dinner. A quick smile flits across Mama's face, then disappears.

The girl is back in a minute. "My mom said for you to pin this on me, Willa. She said she couldn't get it straight."

Mama wipes her hands, goes over to her and takes the corsage, carefully pinning it to the wide collar. I can see it's made of three tiny white roses and lots of ribbon streamers hanging down.

"Thanks," the girl says, smoothing her hands over the perfect pleats of the blue skirt. As she turns and leaves, I tuck in my white blouse tighter and tug at my skirt.

"What were all those ribbons for?" I ask Mama.

She smiles. "Each one was tied to a sugar cube."

"What? Sugar cubes?"

Mama nods. "For sweet sixteen."

I simply shake my head.

Once everyone arrives, the noise of laughter and conversations seeps around the edges of the swinging kitchen door.

"It sounds like a hundred people," I mutter, but Mama just laughs. "Will all of 'em bring a present?"

"Probably," Mama says.

I think about all those presents and wish I'd worn the necklace Mama Lucy gave me.

I keep washing the dishes Mama brings in. She continues taking out more food, refilling the platters.

The hours pass quickly, and I suddenly realize that the house is quiet again. Mama brings in the platters with the few remaining sandwiches and cookies, and we wrap them up to refrigerate.

Miz Pierce bustles in. "Well, everything went well, I think. You can take the leftovers home, Willa, if you want to."

"Thank you, Miz Pierce." I notice that Mama doesn't look up at Miz Pierce when she talks to her.

"Let me know when you're done, and I'll pay you."

"Yes, ma'am," Mama answers. I'm used to Mama having a strong, sure voice. I feel uncomfortable hearing her talk in this quiet way. Mama and I finish up the cleaning, leaving the kitchen spotless.

As we gather our things to go, the girl comes in. "Thanks, Willa, for your help with my party." She looks toward me. "And, you too," she begins. I can tell she's forgotten my name. "Thanks to you too," she finishes lamely.

"You're welcome." As we leave and start down the driveway I can feel myself relax a little. I'm so glad this day is over.

While we're waiting for the bus Mama says, "Now that weren't so bad, was it? You never had to see none of those white kids."

I look sideways at Mama. "No, I didn't have to see any of them. But, Mama, why do you talk in that way to Miz Pierce?"

She sits back and looks at me hard. "What way?"

"You know, that soft kinda way. That way like she deserves all the respect, not you."

Mama crosses her arms over her chest. "I don't know what you talking about, girl."

"Mama—"

"Just hush. I talk to Miz. Pierce like I talk to any other grown-up."

TURNER

I don't say any more out loud, but I'm thinking that Mama has to know what I mean. It's the way all of us talk to the white folk, and it angers me.

The bus rattles to a stop, and Mama and I get on. We sit in silence all the way home.

The next day I tell Mae all about it as we sit on her porch steps after church.

"Tell me'bout the house and everything."

I tell her all about the day. "But, Mae, what makes me mad is that that girl calls my mama by her first name. Not only that, but Mama has to call her Miss Martha Ann."

"But, Letitia, that's the way life is. That's the way it's always been and always will be."

"It's not right. It's not respectful. Don't you see, Mae? That's the kind of thing they've been talking 'bout at the mass meetings. It just isn't fair. We need to change it."

"I don't think we can."

"Maybe not, but we got to try, at least. You were at the mass meeting. Why don't you see?"

"Yeah, but what happens if we're not successful? Don't you think the whites would be harder on us then?"

"That's exactly why we have to be successful, Mae. We have to march with Dr. King. We need to have everybody."

She nods toward my house across the street. "Do you think your folks would ever march? Would mine?"

She knows the answer to that, and so do I. "Well, no, probably not. But you've heard what Shelley Stewart's been saying on the radio. I think someday all the kids will march. Then maybe our parents will join us."

Mae only shakes her head.

"Come on. Think about it. If all of us kids are marching, you'd march too, wouldn't you?"

"I guess." She shrugs.

"Think of how important it is." I keep pushing her. "It's going to happen, I'm sure. You would be part of history."

Mae laughs at that. I lean back and relax, feeling the spring sunshine on my face.

After a few moments of silence, Mae asks, "What was that girl like? Was she mean?"

I think back. "No, she wasn't mean. She was OK. Even came and thanked us before we left."

"Well, see."

"See what?" My voice sounds harsh. "It's not whether or not people are nice to Negroes. It's a matter of fairness, of justice. We don't have the same rights as whites in this country. You know that as well as I do."

Mae sighs. The truth is we both had thought that was the way life was until Dr. King and Rev. Abernathy and the others started showing us all the unfairness.

"It has to change, Mae. And we have to be the ones to change it."

CHAPTER FOUR

We're on the threshold of freedom. It's been nine years since the Supreme Court Decision. All we've got to do is keep marching.
Rev. Ralph Abernathy, *speech during mass meetings, Birmingham, May 1963*

May 2, 1963
LETITIA
THE MOVEMENT

I hear sounds that make me very uneasy. I don't know if it's 'cause of the dozens, no hundreds, of voices getting louder and louder outside the classroom window. Or maybe my feeling is from the chanting I hear coming from the hall, 'specially 'cause I think I hear Sam's voice: "Gotta go, Mr. Johnson, gotta go, gotta go, gotta go." I can picture Mr. Johnson out there, standing with arms folded over his chest saying, "No. You cannot leave the school." Principal R. C. Johnson, he's the man. Like, he's larger than life to us, respected, loved, feared—but this time, this crazy moment in time, there is something even more. Whatever it is, I feel myself trembling as I turn to look out the window.

Then I see it.

"It's Time"

Stark black lettering on the white sign outside the chain-link fence at our all-black Parker High School. The young men don't say a word, just hold up that sign. They don't need to say anything. That message shouts itself to us. Two simple words that could change the world, and I'm part of it. I feel proud, prouder

31

than when I won the class spelling bee, or when Sam used to ride me around on his bike's handlebars. Then, I had felt like a smile was growing big inside me, bigger and bigger until it swelled so big it burst into a happy laugh. But this, this is even more than that.

It's time! Yes, it really is time.

Mae and I talked about it on the way to school this morning.

"I'm sure today's the day," I told Mae right off.

Her eyes flashed with excitement. "How come?"

"Didn't you listen to Shelley Stewart?"

She shook her head. "I didn't have time. Had to iron my blouse."

"He said, 'All right, kids, there's gonna be a party in the park. And don't forget your toothbrushes because luncheon will be served.' And we all know what that means. Be ready to go to jail. Be ready."

I remembered feeling a surge of excitement like the first thought when you wake up and realize it's your birthday. It's a good feeling, a special feeling. We're gonna do it, march in protest against all the injustices, all the oppressive rules, all the hurts. That's what Dr. King told us. Sure, deep inside I know Mama and Daddy are afraid of the protesting even though they want the changes to happen, but Rev. Bevel, Dr. King, Rev. Shuttlesworth, all of them give us kids the strength. I don't know a single friend who won't march. Even Mae got convinced.

My excitement makes me feel all jittery, like I'm about to jump outta' my skin. All of a sudden, though, something else, something small and wiggly enters. And even though I try to push that new feeling away, it stays—a little shadow of fear. No one else seems afraid, but I bet there's a little of that inside each of us.

I look around. I see my classmates gathering by the large open windows, some climbing through. My glance swings to Miz Archer standing at the blackboard, her back to us. Is she deaf?

32

How can she ignore what's happening? It's like everything's in slow motion. She stands there rigidly in her sensible brown suit. Her hand slows as she's writing the assignment. She holds the chalk suspended on the last word, but still she keeps her back to us as one after another of us starts toward the open windows. Like she's holding her breath. You know those times when you get a flash of understanding? Well, that's when I realize something. All our teachers at Parker High School, why, their jobs depend on the white school board, so they never could show their support any other way.

I rush to the windows. My breaths come so fast, and my hands are sweaty. Outside, boys and girls are shoving, pushing against the fence that holds them back until it bends more and more with the weight of students clambering over it.

I'm ready. My toothbrush and comb are tucked in my pocket. All the words I've been listening to for weeks at the mass meetings ring through my heart and give me courage. Rev. Abernathy said we are on the threshold of freedom. Dr. King, he told us there is power in unity, power in numbers. We kids have become that power. I swallow back that little shadow of fear, and now I'm really not afraid. The words Mama Lucy always tells me are in my mind. "*Girl,*" she'd say. "*Girl, life ain't a bit fair or just for us coloreds, but you always got a choice. Your choice is how you gonna take it. You got to stand up proud for who you are, who your kinfolks be, where you come from, and go on to make the best life you can. That's all there is, baby girl. That's it.*" Well, Mama Lucy, I'm ready.

I scramble onto the windowsill with the others, feeling the warm brush of the brick against my bare legs, and drop to the hard, dusty ground. That old fence can't hold back the students flowing out, striding with purpose toward the Sixteenth Street Baptist Church, singing, belting out the words with each step, stronger, stronger.

"We are fighting for our freedom. We shall not be moved. We are fighting for our freedom. We shall not be moved."

Mae's beside me, and I grab her hand; we laugh out loud as we sing.

"*Just like a tree, planted by the water, we shall not be moved.*"

I can hardly believe what I'm seeing. Young people come from every direction, hundreds and hundreds, swarming toward the church. Excitement shimmers in the air. I don't think anything can stop us.

We march past houses where many of us live, those small, whitewashed homes with tiny front yards and the even smaller shotgun houses with the peeling paint and drooping steps. We go by the grocery store, the dry cleaners, the juke joint, the café, and there are grown-ups in the doorways, clapping for us, cheering us on.

"Why aren't they coming too?" I wonder out loud.

Mae glances at me. "Why do you think? If they got jobs, they're probably working for some white man. You think they could risk marching? No way."

Sometimes Mae gets things better than I do. Lately, 'cause of the mass meetings at our churches, though, I'm beginning to understand so much. Rev. Bevel would talk to us and make us see all of the wrongs we had assumed were a normal way of life: not being allowed to use the public library; using hand-me-down textbooks thrown out by the white schools, lots of times with bad, racial hate-words penned in them; having to go in a back door to order at a restaurant and take the food outside. I'd always believed my parents when they said they were too busy to go to Kiddieland, the amusement park. Rev. Bevel dared to tell us that we couldn't enter 'cause of our skin color. When I learned these hard truths I got so mad I felt like I would explode.

The moist heat of the morning moves against my skin like loving hands holding me close. I breathe in the heavy, sweet scent of honeysuckle from some nearby fence. We cover the few blocks between Parker High School and the Sixteenth Street Church fast. The sound of so many shoes slapping the sidewalk forms a beat with the singing, and that rhythm moves us forward. I take in all the familiar landmarks: Kelly Ingram Park, Louie's Grill, The Social Cleaners. I marvel as students come from all directions, singing and chanting. The church is soon packed.

Rev. Bevel stands before us, our leader, our mentor, his familiar cap perched on the back of his shaved head. He told us it was a Jewish yarmulke. I remember 'cause it's such a funny word. He's a tall man, younger than Dr. King and Rev. Abernathy, with an oval face and these big, dark eyes. He never stands still as he preaches to us, pacing and gesturing with the enthusiasm that seems to fill him. We love him, love the way he talks to us, pulls us together, makes us more than we are.

We shall overcome. We shall overcome. We shall overcome someday.

"Do you think we'll have to go to jail?" Mae whispers.

I pause. I can't imagine what jail is like. "I don't know. But if we do, it's gonna be OK. Don't worry." The truth is that my words sound a whole lot braver than I feel. I grasp my hands together so she doesn't see them trembling.

A hush falls over all of us as Rev. Bevel raises his arm. "It's D-day, children. Are y'all with me? Are you ready to march?"

He's talking right to me. His words slam inside me, fill my heart and lungs till I'm bursting, and I have to shout with the others, "Yeah! I'm with you! I'm ready!" I reach up, reach for whatever is ahead.

"Are you ready?" he shouts again.

We roar our agreement, and the sound booms throughout the church. We jump to our feet, clapping and shouting.

"Remember your training. If the police stop you, kneel down and pray. We must be nonviolent. No matter what they do, they cannot stop us."

Cheers and amens burst in the air.

"They cannot stop us because God is with us, and we shall overcome!"

Standing and swaying together the words come as one clear

voice: *We shall overcome. We shall overcome. We shall overcome someday.*

The trembling in my body stops. I see Mae square her shoulders and raise her chin. I take a deep breath and smile at Mae. OK. I'm ready.

Rev. Bevel raises his arms again and the group sits and gets quiet. "Now, before we go, all of y'all pass by these tables and empty your pockets of anything that might be a weapon, any knives, screwdrivers, even your pens and pencils. We are peaceful. We are nonviolent. If they strike at you, turn the other cheek. Do you remember?"

"Yes!" The shouts bounce from the rafters.

"Are you with me?"

None of us stay in our seats as the singing starts. I feel my body sway with the music, sway with the mass of people.

Ain't gonna let nobody turn me around. Ain't gonna let nobody, Lordy, turn me around.

Sam is in the first group out the door, but Mae and I both get bumped toward the back. I don't care, though, 'cause we're all part of it, all of us together. My breath's coming in gasps. My heart, it's just beating faster, but I feel like everyone's heart is beating with the same rhythm, everyone's breath is keeping the same pace. Sure, before we got to the church, I thought about what Mama and Daddy might say, but right now it doesn't matter. Nothing matters except going forward.

Ain't gonna let nobody turn me around. Ain't gonna let nobody, Lordy, turn me around—

Finally our turn comes. Mae and I march through the church door holding our heads high, smiling and singing. Our clear, strong voices carry us forward.

CHAPTER FIVE

Frankly, compared to other places, there's no racial unrest in Birmingham.
Gov. George C. Wallace, *televised remark during Birmingham civil rights campaign, May 1963*

May 2, 1963
LETITIA
THE MOVEMENT

"Move along." "Keep going, niggers." The police herd another group, who'd been marching east toward City Hall, into school buses. The police are big, gruff. They push the marchers with their forearms. They raise their nightsticks as if to strike. I watch the kids, who keep smiling and waving, who keep singing. It's like watching those newsreels of the Nashville sit-ins that Rev. Bevel showed us. Nothing seems like it's really happening right here in front of me, right here in Birmingham.

"Are they sending them back to school?" I ask.

"No way," a boy behind me replies. "They's headed to jail."

Jail! I almost stumble when he says the word "jail." Such a harsh, scary word. Mae grabs my arm, and we keep walking south toward the business district. I watch the faces of those on the bus, laughing and still singing. Our group's instructions are to head to Woolworth's to try to sit at the lunch counter, so we go south instead of heading east toward City Hall like most of the groups.

Police and firemen swarm over the area, and, Lordy, that's more white faces than I've ever seen in one place. Some of the police are just standing 'round, smoking, holding their guns as loose as I carry my books to school. Others yell and push, sending people this way and that.

"Stop right there," I hear them shout at the group right in front of us. "Where's your parade permit?" "You're under arrest." "Move it, nigger." Our group hesitates. We feel ourselves being pushed back as the orderly parade in front of us becomes a milling mass prodded and shoved by the police using their batons.

The adults in the park yell stuff back. "Get out of our neighborhood." "We'll march if we want to. Try and stop us." "We demand equal rights." So much noise. But we all start walking again and singing. Paddy wagons and buses fill up with protesters, take off, and others come back for more. I am amazed at the enthusiasm of the kids as they're pushed and lifted into the backs of the paddy wagons. They fill the bench seats along the sides, and the police slam and lock the double rear doors. I see the faces of kids, a few I know, through the iron mesh of the back window. Somehow, though, our group gets through, and we go on the few blocks to Woolworth's.

I always love it when Mama takes us to Woolworth's. We don't come downtown very much, but when we do, we always go to Woolworth's. Now, though, on this warm May morning I remember things as they really had been.

One time we were walking toward Woolworth's with Mama when a group of white ladies came out. Mama pulled us to the side and even stepped off the sidewalk to make room for them. They never said thank you or even looked at us. When we'd get to the store I'd look at all the shiny jewelry, the scarves, and those pretty plastic flowers shaped like a cross to put on people's graves. The saleslady followed us around so closely. I thought she did that in case we wanted to make a purchase, but after all I've learned lately, I'll bet she thought we were gonna steal something. Sometimes, I wish I hadn't learned so much. I used to feel good about life. Now, these thoughts only make me angry.

I turn to Mae. "You know those ice cream sundaes? The

ones with the whipped cream and chocolate syrup and the cherry on top that they serve at the lunch counter?"

Mae nods. Who didn't see those delicious treats being served and know they weren't for Negroes?

"The first thing I'm gonna do will be order me one of those sundaes." I think about those yummy-looking treats as we approach the wide front doors.

Before we left the church, they'd given us these signs to hold up, signs on heavy, white paper. They say things like "Equal Rights Now" and "End Segregation." Mine says "Birmingham Merchants Unfair" and Mae's reads "Civil Rights for All." There are several stern-looking white men standing in front of the doors, arms crossed, barring entrance. We all are holding these signs high now as our spokesman requests that we be served at the lunch counter.

"Y'all go on home," one man says. "You got no business here." I notice the perspiration dripping off his bald head. He pulls out a white handkerchief and mops his brow.

"We only want a Coca-Cola at the counter." Our leader is slim, but he stands straight and firm. His thin face remains expressionless.

"Well, that's not going to happen. We're closed for today. Y'all don't belong here."

Our leader nods at us, and we know what that means. We're supposed to be nonviolent, just say what we want, but not fight for it, so we all fall into a line and begin walking this oval pattern in front of the store, just like Rev. Bevel told us. Someone starts singing, and we all join in, singing softly.

Woke up this morning with my mind stayed on freedom,
Woke up this morning with my mind stayed on freedom,
Woke up this morning with my mind stayed on freedom,
Hallelujah.

The marching 'round doesn't seem hard at first, but after a little while my feet hurt, and my arms ache from carrying the sign. I remember being told that we probably wouldn't get in, but after seeing so many others getting arrested earlier, I feel confused. I know I don't really want to go to jail, but I thought we were gonna do something great, something really important.

"Mae." I lean closer toward her so she can hear me. "This walking 'round in circles doesn't accomplish anything. I'm beginning to be mad about the assignment we got. It doesn't seem fair. I'd rather be back in school."

Mae glances back at me. "I agree."

But we keep on walking in that big circle.

I don't know how long we've been picketing Woolworth's. It seems like hours, but I know it's not really that long. Some newspaper people came 'round and took some pictures. Finally, our leader says it's OK to head back to the church.

"I can't believe we weren't arrested," I mutter as we scuff along, our rolled-up signs resting loosely in our arms.

Mae nods. "Yeah, but I'm glad, aren't you?"

"I guess; still—" I sigh.

She looks at me in surprise. "Letitia Robinson, I can't believe you. Do you really want to go to jail?"

"Well, just 'cause everyone else is. I mean, what did we accomplish carrying these signs to Woolworth's? Nothing. We didn't do a thing to help the Movement."

I can see that my words hit home. That must be exactly what Mae was thinking. Could it be that of all the hundreds of kids marching today, we're the only ones who didn't achieve anything? We walk in silence the rest of the way to the church. Sometimes disappointment just takes your words away. The crowds have thinned out, today's protest over. Rev. Bevel himself greets the marchers, shaking hands, patting shoulders. "Good job, good job," he keeps repeating.

"We didn't get in," a girl I don't know tells him, shaking her head sadly.

"Now, you know that doesn't matter. The point is the reporters saw it all. They're gonna tell the rest of America. The day will come when you will get in, and you'll sit at the lunch counter and you will be served. That would never happen if you hadn't gone today. You marched for the Movement, Sister. So, thank you, Brothers and Sisters, thank you."

I look at Mae, and we smile at each other. That's why we love Rev. Bevel so much. He reaches inside us and fills us with strong, good feelings. Those feelings that Rev. Bevel gives us last until I get home.

I have such mixed emotions as I get nearer my house. Inside, my thoughts are still churning up with pride and excitement, yet, now, now I have to face Mama and Daddy. One last look over my shoulder at Mae as she heads into her house, then I reach for the doorknob. The front door flies open, and Mama pulls me inside. I can feel the trembling of Mama's hand as if her body can't hold in all she's feeling.

"Sam's in jail! Pastor just called and told us all about the marching. He saw Sam being arrested and he saw you there too. What in God's good name were you thinking, girl?" Mama cries. "You lost your mind? Don't you know you gonna get 'spelled from school? How's that gonna look on your record? Don't you want—" Tears of anger and relief choke her last words. Mama steps back, wringing her hands.

I think of my mama as always neat, but now? Now, she looks like a skein of yarn coming unraveled. Her black hair is all flyaway wisps. Her lipstick on her full lips is smeared, her posture bent over.

"Mama—" One look at Mama's face stops me cold. Her eyes are filled with fear, her face all splotchy. I've seen Mama showing emotion lots of times. That's how Mama is. Everyone's seen her during church services, her arms raised to Jesus, tears streaming down her face, words of praise and amens, calling Jesus's name. But this emotion! This emotion hurls itself at me. This is different from anything I've ever known.

I know my mama, 'course I do. What she cares most about in this whole world is her children—me, Sam, and Etta. So, I knew she'd be upset some. How many times have I heard her say,

TURNER

"There's nothing more important than family. Don't you ever forget that." How many times have I heard her talk about her own family, her growing-up years? *Yeah, I knew she'd be unhappy with Sam and me. I knew she'd be upset, but this upset? Lordy, Lordy.*

Mama starts again. "You know I work for Miz Pierce. You think she gonna keep me knowing my children be protesting, going to jail? What you—"

Just then Daddy strides in from the back, slamming the door behind him. He takes my arms in his big hands and shakes me. My bones are rattling inside me. I've never seen him so mad. His chin juts forward, his dark eyes blazing. When he lets go, he turns and slams a fist into the wall. When he turns back to me, I shrink back. My arms still burn from his grip. Suddenly I wish this morning had never happened. No, that's not true! *If only they understood.*

"Why, Letitia, why?" His voice cuts through me, and I start to cry.

"But, Daddy, wait. Listen. Everyone went. We all marched. We had to, Daddy. Don't you see?" The tears keep flowing. "We had to."

"No," his voice is fierce sounding. "No, you didn't *have* to."

Wiping my tears with the back of my hand, I look straight at him. "Everything I learned at the mass meetings, everything my friends talk 'bout, all of it adds up to something stronger than any Sunday school lesson." I pause, and then I dare to say it. "The Movement is even stronger than any rules you've ever given me, Daddy. It's more. More."

Daddy takes a deep breath, looks away, then shakes his head. "I could lose my job, honey. Don't you know that? We make the white boss mad, and we lose everything I done worked for. Everything."

Mama turns and walks toward the kitchen, wiping her eyes on her apron.

I gulp back my crying and square my shoulders. It isn't their anger that surprises me. It's their fear; it's fear that is fueling their anger.

"Daddy, listen. You heard Dr. King. You and Mama went to the mass meetings too. We have to make it stop sometime. And now's the time." I swallow and look at him. I've always thought of him as strength, as security, but at this moment, I see something else. I see the fear in his eyes. Even in the face of that, or maybe because of it, I keep trying to explain. "At the mass meetings, I don't know. It's like the idea of the Movement swells up inside me until it's bigger than me, bigger than our family, that it's something for all people, like they've been trying to tell us. And I know being in it is what I have to do." Daddy just turns, shaking his head, and goes to see Mama in the kitchen. Now that I see their fear it scares me.

That evening when we're all sitting 'round the supper table the only sounds are the clink of forks against plates, the scrape of passing dishes. It's like if we speak, our feelings would bust out and overwhelm us. The smell of fried catfish hangs heavy in the air. Seems like we all avoid looking at Sam's empty chair, even Mama Lucy. Etta's probably too young to really know what's going on, but she's eating so quietly and her little, round face looks from Mama to Daddy every now and then. Mama keeps pushing her food around her plate, scarcely eating a bite. Sam's always the one to keep our suppertimes lively, always telling something funny that happened at school or jive-talking to tease Daddy.

Lots of folks think Sam is only a clown, but he's always looked out for me and Etta. He's smart too. He'll be the first in the family to finish high school, then he wants to go into the service, and maybe someday get them to pay for his college. I believe he can do it too. *Oh, my gosh. Will his being arrested mess up those plans?*

"Eat your supper, sugar," Mama Lucy urges me.

My attention snaps back to the table. "I'm trying to eat, but it's like there's a knot in my stomach and the food settles in a lump."

"Still, you got to eat," she tells me, so I try. My feet scuff against the worn linoleum floor, but that reminds me too much of the morning's marching so I try to keep them still. I steal a glance at my parents. Fear is wearing them down, sagging their shoulders. I try to swallow a mouthful, but it doesn't go down very well.

Mama slams her fork to the table. "I can't stand it!" Tears pour down her face. "I never thought a child of mine would be in the jail. Jail! What's happening to him, Arthur? What're they doing to our boy?"

Poor Daddy. He's just as upset, but he has to keep calm for Mama. He sighs. "Hush up, woman. He all right. The news said they's over nine hunnerd children arrested, and you know they ain't gonna all fit in the jailhouse. They's over at the juvie hall, and most probably, they's having a big party. After supper I'll go down to the church and find out what's going on. Stop your fretting. Anyways, it's done. There ain't a thing we can do."

Mama simply shakes her head, gets up, and starts clearing off the table. I know what she's thinking. It always comes down to what Daddy said: "There ain't a thing we can do." I keep my eyes down as I stand to help Mama. *That's why we have to march, because it's time for us to finally do something.* I think about this morning, and I wonder why we didn't get arrested. I guess the police were too busy to get everyone.

Today was D-day, but Rev. Bevel told us tomorrow was Double-D-day. This protest is gonna go on and on until something happens. And I'm gonna be part of it.

After supper I go into Mama Lucy's room. I need to talk to someone who might understand. She smiles and pats the bed next to her so I know she's expecting me. She was keeping that warm, safe spot for me.

Even though she's so tiny, I lean my head against her and find strength. She puts her arm around me and that opens me up so everything starts to pour out, all my feelings. "I didn't mean to hurt Mama and Daddy. Will they ever forgive me? Will they forgive Sam? I wonder what's happening to him. Like when anything bad happens, I keep thinking that I wish this never happened, but that's not true. This had to happen. Everyone was marching. I didn't care about Mama and Daddy. They should know we have to march, shouldn't they?"

Mama Lucy listens and listens. Finally, I have no more words. She pats my hand. "You're right, Letitia. You're doing right. It's time. Your folks, they'll come 'round. You do what you need to do."

It seems like hours till Daddy gets back from the church. We hear him coming in the back door, so we go to meet him and sit 'round the kitchen table to hear the news.

"Well, I learned about everything," he reports. "The Movement's gonna get the money to bail out the kids, but it might be a lot of days." Mama puts her hand to her mouth when he says that.

"Dr. King, he talked to us hisself. Dr. King told us not to worry."

"Ha!" Mama spits out. I know she couldn't help herself.

Daddy looks at her quick-like, then goes on. "This is exactly what Dr. King say. He say, 'Don't worry about your children. They doing a job for all America and all mankind.' Weren't that something? He say some important people from the Justice Department are down here to see that the kids are OK. That makes me feel some better."

"But what about Sam?" Mama interrupts.

Daddy nods. "I learned that he at the juvenile hall, not the jail." Mama sits back and lets out a big breath. I feel the same way. Juvie hall's not as bad as jail, I guess. They didn't say anything to the parents about marching tomorrow, but I know we will. I can't believe that Mama and Daddy don't forbid me to go. I believe that they don't think there will be any more marching, but there will be. There has to be.

As I get ready for bed, the house stays strangely quiet. I guess my parents have no words of comfort for each other. Etta holds her stuffed rabbit more tightly than usual and goes softly to bed without any fuss. The whole family is tilting out of kilter. Feelings swirl crazily inside me: worry over Sam, recklessness at daring to go against my parents' wishes, and, I can't deny it, fear. Fear for myself. *Is jail a possibility for me too? 'Course, it is. They all said that—Dr. King, Rev. Bevel, Andrew Young—all of them.*

I look over at Etta, already asleep with her thumb in her mouth. How would she feel with both her brother and sister in jail? Could she ever understand what Sam and I are doing? I turn off the light and climb into bed beside her. I close my eyes and think about the day, the sheet whispering 'round my legs as I get into a comfortable position. I remember what I heard some of the grown-ups saying after one of the meetings. They said that Dr. King wanted to keep all the reporters here, telling about Birmingham, showing how Bull Connor hates the Negroes. Dr. King wants to fill the jails and have the television show all the country so that people will care.

Well, the jails are full. One of the prisoners is my brother. Tomorrow, will another be me? I turn over and try to put the thought out of my mind, hoping for an escape in sleep. Sleep will keep me safe. And finally, after all the tears of this evening, I know the Movement will go on, and I will be part of it.

CHAPTER SIX

These young people are about their Father's business. They are carving a tunnel of hope through the great mountain of despair. They will bring to this nation a newness and a genuine quality and an idealism that is desperately needed.

Dr. Martin Luther King, Jr., *speech at mass meetings, Birmingham, May 3, 1963*

May 2, 1963
MARTHA ANN
OVER THE MOUNTAIN

"No one goes downtown tomorrow!" Martha Ann's father slammed his fist on the table.

Martha Ann looked up in surprise. While she was used to her father's stark orders about their activities, she couldn't imagine what brought on this outburst. "But I just want to go to the Record Rack to use my birthday money to buy the *Surfin' USA* album." Martha Ann exchanged a quick look of confusion with her younger brother, Brad. "It's my money, Daddy."

"This hasn't got anything to do with whose money it is, damn it. This is because I don't want anyone in my family going anywhere near downtown. You hear me!" He dug his fork into his casserole and shoved it into his mouth.

Mrs. Pierce looked as confused as Martha Ann. "Why can't we go downtown, Harold?"

"It's some crazy outside agitators. They've come to Birmingham again, and they got the coloreds all fired up. There could be big trouble."

47

"Why'd they come here, Daddy?" asked Brad, grabbing a second biscuit.

"Who knows? Those communist ba—" Stealing a glance at his wife he changed his wording quickly. "Those bums. Our Negras are just fine the way they are. Everybody knows their place and everything works OK."

"But what do they want?" persisted Martha Ann. She actually had never been around any Negroes except sometimes when she'd see that colored woman who worked for her mom, but they never had much conversation.

Mrs. Pierce laid her hand gently on her husband's arm as she turned toward her daughter. "A law was passed for them to go to school with whites. I think that's what they want," she answered.

"That'll be the day," scoffed Mr. Pierce.

Martha Ann ate a few bites, thinking over what her mother had said. "But why do they want to? I mean, don't they want to keep to themselves, to people like them, just like we do?"

Her mother simply shrugged.

"Can I go to Jimmy's after school tomorrow?" Brad asked, bringing the family back to their usual routine.

Martha Ann glanced at her dad, his elbows on the table, not paying attention to anything but his food. She often wished he was more like her friend Molly's dad, tall and dark haired. Instead, his small, wiry frame was no taller than her mom's. Martha Ann sighed. She had inherited his pale hazel eyes and his sandy blond hair, a shade that some of the girls in her class called "dirty blonde." *Why couldn't I have Mom's dark brown hair and beautiful brown eyes?* Lately, he acted like he was the king and anything he said was the law. He wouldn't let her wear makeup until her mother finally got him to allow her to wear lipstick. He didn't want her to date unless it was a group thing, not that any boy had ever asked her. Still, she hoped that might happen soon. Then, this last year he started getting so mad about things. At first, he only yelled at her mom, but more and more he'd screamed at them too. One time Brad accidently pushed his hand through the screen door. Martha Ann had been afraid he was going to slam Brad against the wall, he had grabbed him so hard. She pushed those thoughts out of her mind.

After dinner, Martha Ann sat at the table working on her math homework. She looked up at her mother untying her apron after putting the last clean dish away. "Mom, those colored people," she began, "they won't come to our school, will they?" Her mother sighed, pulled out the chair next to Martha Ann and sat down. She glanced toward the living room where her husband sat engrossed in a TV show. Pulling a pack of Salems from her pocket, she struck a match and lit her cigarette. Martha Ann watched the wisp of smoke and took in the familiar sweet tobacco scent as she waited for her mother's response.

"Sugar, I can't imagine that it would happen, even though there is a law about it."

"But why are they causing trouble now?"

Mrs. Pierce shook her head. "I don't know why now, honey. Just before Easter the news on the TV said that Martin Luther King fellow was down here leading a protest, and he got arrested. He's the one who's always trying to change things. Maybe they got tired of having to ride in the back of the bus or drink from separate water fountains. Who knows? Sure, Willa comes here twice a week to help me, but she's never said anything about it. There's no reason for us to talk about such as that. I don't know anything about the coloreds. I do know, though, that sometimes fights between Negroes and whites can get violent, so we'd better listen to your daddy and stay away."

"But, Mom—"

Mrs. Pierce pushed her chair back from the table and stood up. "Martha Ann, don't you pay a mind to what's going on with the coloreds. It's nothing to do with us. Have you and Molly decided about which of us is going to carry y'all to Noreen's party Saturday night?"

Martha Ann smiled at her mother. "Will you drive us there?"

"Sure, darlin'. Are you about finished with your homework?"

Martha Ann nodded and turned back to the last of the math problems. At her mother's mention of the party, though, her mind had wandered to a more important subject. *I hope Donald is going to be there. I wonder if he'll ask me to dance this time.*

During her first class the next day, Martha Ann's thoughts slipped to the idea of having Negroes in school with them. *There's not enough room in our school for a whole other school to come in. Does that mean that some of us would have to go to a Negro school? That's impossible. Why are they stirring things up anyway?*

Later, when the lunch bell sounded and students swarmed to the cafeteria, the noise level in the halls rose like an angry cloud of bees lifting off. Martha Ann carried her tray to the usual table where her friends gathered. Talk danced between them, taking them from one topic to another. Of course, the end-of-the-year party was the main subject.

"Carl said he was coming, and he's bringing Tony, Steve, and Larry," commented Sandra, her voice carrying the smugness of insider knowledge.

Martha Ann wanted to ask about Donald, but hesitated. It wasn't smart to reveal too much.

Molly seemed distracted. "Does anyone know what's going to be on that English test Monday?" Heads shook no, and conversation dwindled as the girls picked through their lunches, the golden swirl of mac and cheese, the tinny taste of canned string beans.

"Did you know the Negroes are having a big protest? My dad says we shouldn't go downtown." Martha Ann looked around at her friends, waiting for their reply as silence descended on the group like an unwelcome stranger.

"Who cares?" Sandra said, annoyance edging her voice.

"Well, my mom says they want to come to our schools," Martha Ann persisted.

Sandra paused before taking a bite, the fork halfway to her mouth. "They'd better not try it, that's all I can say."

"I just don't get why they want to. I mean, they have their stuff, and we have ours," Martha Ann continued.

Connie, who usually remained quietly on the outskirts of the group, surprised her by speaking up. "I think it's more than wanting to come to our schools. They want things to be equal, to be fair."

Martha Ann noticed that her friends either ignored what Connie had said or gave her dirty looks. "But, I don't get it. They have everything we have."

Connie shook her head. "If they go to the movies at the Lyric they have to go up the back stairs and sit in the balcony, they can't go to the library, they can't get a Coke or anything downtown like we can."

"Who wants to talk about niggers anyway?" Sandra's voice cut in sharply. She turned to the girl sitting next to her. "What are you wearing to the party Saturday?"

Connie continued eating her lunch, not looking upset that the others cut her off.

Doesn't she care what everyone thinks? Martha Ann wondered. *Connie's parents are known for being real liberal, and I guess Connie is too. But even so, I'd think she wouldn't speak up like that knowing how everyone else feels about Negroes. I'm not sure if I admire her or if I think she's a fool.*

May 3, 1963
LETITIA
THE MOVEMENT

In the morning, I dress carefully in a freshly ironed white blouse and plaid skirt. I again slip my toothbrush and comb into my pocket. As I start out of my room, I turn back and hurry to my bureau, grabbing up a handkerchief and the gold locket Mama Lucy gave me on my birthday. It's become my most cherished possession, not only because a picture of Mama Lucy is inside, but because of the words she said when she gave me the gift.

I think today is the kind of day that I'll need whatever it is my grandmother was talking about. I hope to slip out without seeing Mama or Daddy, but I know that's impossible. Daddy left earlier, as usual, but Mama is still in the kitchen, leaning against the sink drinking her coffee.

"I made you some toast, Letitia. Better eat it."

That's one thing about Mama—no matter how mad or upset she is, she always wants to feed us something.

"Thanks, Mama." She looks tired. I bet she didn't sleep much last night, worrying about Sam. Poor Mama. Poor Sam.

"Mama, I . . . ," I begin, just as she says, "Letitia, . . . "

We laugh, and Mama hugs me. She says softly, "Just remember, your education is the most important thing. Schooling is the only thing that will get you where you need to go. Don't you be risking it foolishly."

I pull back and look at her. "I know, Mama. I gotta go now. Mae'll be waiting."

She nods and pats my arm. "Take the toast with you, honey."

I meet Mae at the corner. She waves the minute she sees me. "You sure look excited," I say.

She laughs. "You look the same." We start out walking, our steps almost bouncing.

"Should we go to school, or just to the church?" asks Mae.

"Let's go by the church first and see if everyone's there. Did you know Sam was arrested? Mama's really upset."

"I think everyone got arrested but us. Maybe today we'll be the ones."

I shake my head. "I don't know if my mama could stand that."

As we get near the church, there's no doubt that students are already gathering there. Inside, the church fills up quickly. Rev. Bevel, Rev. Abernathy, and Andrew Young take turns encouraging us, leading us in prayers and songs.

"We want to be free. Don't you want to be free?" Rev. Abernathy holds up his arms, questioning.

"Yeah," we shout.

"Do you want freedom?"

"Yeah." We clap our hands as we shout at the top of our lungs.

He kinda chuckles. "Why don't you say something when I'm talking to you?" And we all laugh.

We pray, we sing, and we're ready to go.

"Yesterday was victory, children. Victory! Do you know why?" James Bevel's voice holds us, brings us together, gives our very breath meaning. "I'll tell you why. The people of this great country weren't caring about what was happening to you down here in Birmingham, Alabama. They weren't caring that you can't walk freely about. They weren't caring that the white man calls your daddy and your granddaddy 'boy.' They weren't caring that you can't eat in any restaurant you want, that you can't stay in any hotel you want. But they care now. They care because of you children. Last night as they sat in their comfortable homes watching the TV, they saw the reports of you, the children. All over this country people learned about what was happening in Birmingham, Alabama, all because of you. And what were you children doing?"

I jump up with the others. "Marching! We was marching!"

Rev. Bevel's smile is beaming at us as he claps his hands. "That's right. You were marching. You were not afraid. You were peacefully marching for the rights of all Negroes, and that Bull Connor arrested you! Arrested children and put them in jail. And the whole world saw it. So now they care about what's happening in Birmingham, Alabama, and you made them care. And you'll make them care again today. Are you with me?"

I put away all thoughts of the anguish on Mama's face, the fear Daddy has about his job. For a moment I think about Sam, but the roar of those around me drowns it out. I have one thought: *I have to do this; I am part of this.*

"We're with you!" we shout.

We are to go out in groups of fifty at a time. We pass the tables, emptying our pockets of the usual things that might be considered weapons. Singing and smiling, we start out, down the steps of the church, past the few hundred spectators cheering us on in Kelly Ingram Park. Rev. Bevel told us that reporters and TV people are here from all over the country, and that's what the Movement wanted. I see men with big cameras. I wonder if I'll be in any of the pictures.

Today there are more police, and fire trucks are set up at the corners. "I've never seen so many white folk 'round here," comments Mae. The truth is that in our fifteen years, we almost never have been with whites. I'm beginning to know what a cocoon I've been in. We live in our own world, a close-knit world. We have all these strict grown-ups around, from our parents to our teachers and our pastor. And we look at them with respect. The strictness of my parents about where I could go and what I could do kept me from facing the often-painful experiences I'd learned about at the mass meetings. I've come to realize that the rigid rule about never going past Seventeenth Street was 'cause Negroes are not welcome in the white downtown, that the reason I'm not allowed to go to the downtown public library was really because Negroes aren't allowed in, that I'm not allowed to ride a city bus without Mama or Daddy to keep me from mistakenly sitting in the wrong area. They wrapped us in a blanket of security, but it kept our world small, unaware. Now I see and it makes me mad.

The marchers start down Fifth Avenue toward downtown. I can see every emotion around me: excitement, joy, pride, arrogance, and fear. And I feel every one of those emotions. A rush of something surges through me, fills me with the excitement that's in the air around me. I feel the thrill of being part of something so important. Important not only for us, but now I see it's for the whole country. And yet, my stomach knots, my hands perspire, and my throat catches as I sing. I put my hand to the chain around my neck and clasp the locket firmly. OK, Mama Lucy. I know you'd be marching today if you were me.

We march another fifty feet. "Stop!" The voice of Bull Connor roars above the singing. "Don't go any farther, or we'll turn the fire hoses on y'all." This feared white man stands there in his dark suit with his hands on his hips. His thin dark tie looks like an upside-down exclamation point against his white shirt, ending at his wide neck. I've heard so much about this man and his cruelty, and I think he looks like a man who could be cruel, though I expected him to be taller. He wears a dark hat with a striped band pushed back from his wide forehead, and his dark-rimmed glasses and full face make me think of a toad.

We get as far as Seventeenth Street, the invisible line that divides blacks from downtown. We hesitate, then move on.

The fire hoses are spread in lines all over the streets from those big fire trucks.

"Open them up," Connor shouts.

The hoses come alive, jerk and roll as they fill with water. At first the fire hoses aren't on full force, although I see many of the marchers stumble as the water slaps against them. Then, the hoses go to full force. People are knocked off their feet. Kids are thrown up against the buildings, tossed down the street like small trash. A man in a white shirt and then a woman in a flowered dress begin yelling at the firemen and police, and the hoses sweep 'round on them. A fireman yells, "Get more hoses! They're throwing bricks!" People are screaming, children crying, rocks and bottles shower down from the top of the buildings onto the police and firemen. Officers shout, "Knock the niggers down!" Everything swirls in a mad rush: bodies, paper, clothes. The hoses swing around violently.

I don't know which way to turn, where to go. I look up to see what to do, and the water slams against my chest. I'm thrown backward. The spray catches what little sunlight there is, cascading a silvery mist sparkling above me. For a moment, it's like

TURNER

everything is in slow motion, and then chaos. My heartbeat races and a scream of terror starts, but for a second I can't hear anything but the rush of water. That water is like a monster. I can't fight against it. I slam against a doorway of a brick building and gasp to get a breath in the barrage of water. The water spins me on, my skin burning as I scrape against the brick wall. The pressure of that water pushes, pushes. My chest feels crushed. For a moment I can't see, can't breathe. The chain of the locket is torn from my neck. I reach and reach for it, but the water swirls it away. With what feels like my last ounce of breath, screams tear from my throat, "No! No!"

CHAPTER SEVEN

Negroes and whites will not segregate together as long as I am Commissioner.
Eugene "Bull" Connor, *"Integration: Bull at Bay," Newsweek,*
April 15, 1963

May 3, 1963
LETITIA
THE MOVEMENT

It seems like an hour since the fire hoses first sprayed us, but it's probably only minutes. I lean against the building for a while. I can't move. My back is against the rough brick wall, and my skin burns from being scraped along it.

"Mae, where are you?" I call as I try to wring out my plaid skirt. It's torn and hanging down, and my slip shows through on that side. My face is wet from the water dripping off my hair, and I'm crying from anger. My heart is beating wildly, and I'm trembling all over. I can't quite catch my breath as I choke and gasp.

Mae is not far away, bent over, coughing and sputtering.

"Mae, are you all right?"

She glances toward me, her hand against the building. She looks like that's the only thing holding her up. "I . . . I think so. Are you?"

"I guess so, but I lost my chain. The one my Mama Lucy gave me."

"I can't believe they would turn fire hoses on us." Mae's words come out between tears and coughs.

I stand straighter and look around. I see Damon a few feet away. He looks at me, and I burn with shame that he can see my underwear. He turns away as I try to pull my skirt around me again. Our park, the wide streets, the sidewalks all are a war zone like I've only seen in the movies before. There is no more orderly march, simply masses of people milling around; many look as dazed as I feel. There's noise, but it's not all together like our singing was. It's people shouting and crying, and the harsh yells of the police and firemen have sharp edges, like knives being thrown into the crowd, and the breaking of glass from bottles people are throwing at the law. I feel dizzy. Nothing makes any sense.

I don't think my body can hold any more, but right next to the anger and resentment, I feel something even stronger. I am filled with sadness. White people must truly hate Negroes. They don't care if we're grown-ups or children, good people or bad people. They hate us. Before it was only like smoke. Now, though, it's a fire that has scorched me through and through. And it's a burn that will never heal.

Mae reaches for me and we hug, holding each other up, weeping together.

"Let's go home," she says.

I think about searching for my locket, but, really, I only want to go home. For a moment I wonder what Mama Lucy will say about all this. We slowly make our way back toward our houses through the noise and wet.

"Look out!" Mae yells. I can hardly hear her, but she yanks me toward her.

Huge dogs strain against their leashes. I can't move for a minute as I stare at the bared teeth of a snarling dog. I've never been so frightened. Mae keeps pulling me to the opposite side of the street.

"Dogs! Dogs? Fire hoses and now dogs." I glance at Mae and shake my head. I don't understand this hatred. I can't even look back to see what kind of man would use a dog against me, a fifteen-year-old, sopping wet, scared girl. And, yes, a Negro girl. I try to hold back my tears because I know if I start to cry, my sobbing won't stop.

We step over broken glass and bricks, avoiding the police and firemen, staying away from the water sloshing its way along the edges of the street. Only moments ago we walked out of the church, happy, proud, singing, but now? How can things change so fast? What will Mama and Daddy say? I don't care. I only want to go home. We trudge along, and it never seemed so far to my house as it does now. My clothes weigh a ton, they're so full of water. My shoes squish with every step. Mae and I don't say a word. What good would words do, anyway?

When I walk in the house, Mama comes from the kitchen. She takes one look at me and opens her arms. In two quick strides I run to her, and she holds me tight. "Baby," is all she says, "baby," as she strokes my hair.

Even though it's Saturday, I know there will continue to be demonstrations today and 'course, there are. But I also think they'll end in the early afternoon, like all the others. I wait till about three o'clock then call Mae and ask her to go with me to hunt for my locket.

Mae and I poke through the debris and water from another day of hosing attacks. "You'll never find that locket, Letitia. Why you even trying?"

I'm not sure I can explain, but I try. "All my life Mama Lucy has talked to me about the struggles of the Negroes. She told me how our ancestor came from Senegal in Africa, how he was captured by another tribe when they raided his village, then sold as a slave and brought here in those terrible slave ships. He was only a boy, the age we are now. She told me how he was bought by an awful mean master when he got to South Carolina, and that he tried lots of times to escape, and they finally cut his heel real bad so he could hardly walk after that."

"What's that gotta do with your locket?"

"Everything. Mama Lucy said his strong spirit made him

59

survive every terrible thing that happened, and that same spirit was in her and in my daddy and in me. The locket is s'posed to remind me about that."

We spend nearly an hour kicking through all the mess left in the gutters 'round Kelly Ingram Park. I can't believe how much trash there is: paper, broken bottles, our torn signs, cans, bricks, pieces of fabric that I guess are from when the force of the water tore at people's clothes. My hands are caked with mud and blood from where I cut myself on a broken bottle. Being here brings back all the bad feelings from yesterday, but I keep searching and searching.

"It's got to be here." I work a little faster, stirring up the mess with a stick.

Then I kick some broken glass aside and see something shiny under the leaves. I grab it real quick, and, sure enough, it's my locket.

"I told you!" I jump up and down, hugging Mae. She only laughs at me, but I know she's glad I found it. As we walk back home, I share some more of what Mama Lucy had told me.

"Whenever Mama Lucy tells about our ancestors, she'd say, 'Now, 'member this, sugar. You got to 'member where you come from so you know where you is going.' I never really understood that part, but I know it's important. That's why I got to keep this locket 'round my neck where I can feel it being a part a' me."

When I go to bed I like the warmth of Etta's little body snuggling near me. After all that happened yesterday I move close, like I'm reaching for anything that's part of our normal, regular life. I think about Mama Lucy and all she means to me. I love to hear the stories she tells me. Then my thoughts wander to all the little things like how she'll brush my hair without pulling so hard that it hurts, the yummy bread pudding she makes, things like that. I do worry about her though. This diabetes is a bad thing, I know. A little while ago she talked about dying. She said, "Now, sugar, when I die, I don't want you grieving on and on, hear me? I want

you to 'member all the things I told you, and when you're think-
ing about them, it's like I'll still be there, see? As long as someone's
'membering you, you never die." That's sort of true, but I would
really miss feeling her arms 'round me, smelling that vanilla smell
of her. As I nestle into my comfortable position, I imagine her
holding me close. That helps me forget the bad feelings, at least a
little bit.

May 1963
MARTHA ANN
OVER THE MOUNTAIN

That evening, after her father got home with the paper, Martha
Ann plopped down on the couch and absently picked up the
front section of the news. Her dad busied himself with his beer
and the television, that fifteen minutes of Huntley and Brinkley.
Nothing on the front page caught her attention, so she turned to
the next. The headline immediately drew her gaze: "Fire hoses,
police dogs used to halt downtown Negro demonstrations."
    She glanced quickly at her dad. *So, he was right. We*
shouldn't have gone downtown. She returned to the paper and
began reading.

> ABOUT 100 YOUTHFUL NEGRO DEMONSTRATORS, SINGING
> AND STRUTTING, WERE DISPERSED WITH FIRE HOSES AND
> POLICE DOGS THIS AFTERNOON AS NEW MARCHES WERE
> ATTEMPTED ON THE DOWNTOWN AREA NEAR KELLY IN-
> GRAM PARK. . . .
>   THE MARCHERS WERE ACCOMPANIED BY A CROWD
> OF 400 TO 600 BOISTEROUS NEGROES WHO FOLLOWED
> ALONG BEHIND THEM.
>   MANY FIREMEN, REPORTERS, AND POLICEMEN
> WERE HIT WHEN NEGROES HURLED BRICKS AND BOTTLES.
>   FIREMAN, WITH THE FOGGING NOZZLES ON,
> TURNED WATER ON THE SEVERAL GROUPS OF MARCHERS

AND A CROWD IN THE PARK, WHEN THEY REFUSED TO DIS-
PERSE.

THE CROWD THINNED OUT AND FINALLY DISPERSED
WHEN POLICE DOGS WERE CALLED OUT. A NEGRO LEAD-
ER URGED THE CROWD TO EITHER RETURN TO THE SIX-
TEENTH STREET BAPTIST CHURCH, WHERE THE MARCH-
ERS STARTED, OR GO HOME. . . .

AFTER THE FIRST GROUP OF ABOUT 40 CARD-CAR-
RYING NEGRO DEMONSTRATORS MARCHED AWAY FROM
THE CHURCH AT ABOUT 12:30 P.M., ANOTHER GROUP OF
SINGING, KNEELING AND THEN RISING NEGROES STARTED
ACROSS KELLY INGRAM PARK TOWARD FIFTH AVENUE.

FIREMAN WAITED THERE WITH FIRE HOSES, AND
WHEN MARCHERS REFUSED TO DISPERSE POLICE CAPT. G.
V. EVANS GAVE AN ORDER TO SPRINKLE THEM WITH WA-
TER.

MOST SPECTATORS GAVE GROUND, BUT ABOUT 10
NEGROES REFUSED TO BUDGE AND SAT ON THE SIDEWALK.
FIREMAN THEN TURNED THE WATER ON FULL.

THE GROUP GOT UP AND RAN.

THE CHANTING NEGROES GATHERED IN THE PARK
BEGAN TO BOO POLICE AND FIREMAN AND SHOWERED
THE OFFICERS WITH ROCKS, BRICKS, AND BOTTLES. "FIRE
HOSES, POLICE DOGS USED TO HALT DOWNTOWN NEGRO
DEMONSTRATION," THE BIRMINGHAM NEWS, MAY 3, 1963

Martha Ann stared at the picture beside the article. Two
children, a boy who looked about her age and a little girl, stood
with their backs against a chain-link fence. A heavily armed
policeman stood facing them. The caption read "SIX-YEAR OLD
GIRL AWAITS TURN TO ENTER PADDY WAGON." And
underneath that, "She was among hundreds of demonstrators arrested."

Martha Ann shivered. *A six-year-old girl! Going to jail!
What were they thinking, putting that little girl out there?*

*While we were laughing and talking with our friends, kids
our age were getting sprayed with fire hoses just on the other side of
Red Mountain. I can't imagine that. Why would anyone want to be*

part of that? I wonder if that girl of Willa's was there.

"What's so interesting in that paper, honey?" Her dad's voice startled her, bringing her back to their familiar living room.

"Oh, nothing. I was looking for the comics."

"Well, you can read them later. Hand me the paper now so's I can get it read before your mom calls us to supper."

The next Saturday afternoon Martha Ann sat on her front steps, the oppressive heat making her feel lazy. The azaleas were in full bloom, and bees buzzed busily around the confederate jasmine at the side of the house. She hadn't heard her father's angry voice at night in over a week. *Maybe everything's OK again.* Even so, she was afraid to hope the bad times had passed. There had been lulls before, then suddenly the shouting would start again. She never knew what might set it off. That was what kept her uneasy.

She spied Connie riding her Schwinn bike down the road and waved at her to stop.

"Want some sweet tea?" she suggested.

"Sure." Connie set the kickstand in place and waited while Martha Ann brought out the two glasses.

"Whatcha' been doing?" asked Connie.

"Nothing. I'm wanting to go downtown, but Daddy won't let us 'cause of the Negroes."

Connie nodded as she sipped the tea, the glass sweating coolness in her hand.

Martha Ann looked at her friend quietly for a moment. "Connie, weren't you afraid that Sandra and them might never talk to you again after what you were saying about the coloreds at the lunch table?"

"My daddy says that if people don't like you 'cause you have a different opinion than they do, well, they aren't the kind of friends you want anyway."

Martha Ann frowned. "But if no one at school will be your friend, you'd be so lonely. If Sandra decides not to like you, she can make the whole class not like you."

"Oh, I don't think so."

Martha Ann looked hard at Connie. *Does she really believe that?* Connie seemed to read her thoughts and simply shrugged her shoulders.

"Do you know any Negroes?" asked Martha Ann. "Do you know why they're causing all this trouble? We have a colored woman, Willa, who helps my mom some, but Mom won't ask her anything about the demonstrations."

Connie shook her head. "I don't really know any, but my daddy says they're tired of being treated like second-class citizens. He says it's only a matter of time until everything will be equal between the races."

"But how can it? How can we change from the way things have always been?"

"He didn't tell me that, but he says it'll be a mess for a while."

"Do you think they'll come over the mountain and bother us here?" That familiar knot of concern that recently had become a companion made its way into Martha Ann's stomach. "The Hansons are putting burglar bars on their windows."

"My daddy doesn't think they'll come over the mountain. But he says the riots will continue until the Negroes get what they want."

"But what *do* they want? I don't really understand." Martha Ann brushed away an annoying fly.

Connie shrugged as she sipped the last of her tea. "You should come to my house sometime and ask my daddy. He knows all about it, I think."

Martha Ann sighed. "Well, I don't like it. I want the fighting to stop." She looked off toward downtown, wondering when she could use her birthday money for that album. She thought about the violence going on just over the mountain. "I just want to feel safe again."

The next morning, Martha Ann looked at herself in the mirror as she got ready for Sunday school and church. She liked the way she looked in her pink sundress and Sunday shoes.

"Martha Ann, Brad. Y'all come on, or we'll be late," her mother called to them. Martha Ann smiled. Her mother said the same thing every Sunday morning, and they had never been late. She picked up her white straw purse and gloves and hurried to join her parents.

Old Miz Patterson taught the Sunday school lesson, as usual. Her white, wispy hair formed a halo around her head, with her blue velvet hat, secured by two long pearl-tipped hatpins, topping it all. Martha Ann and Molly tried not to smirk at Miz Patterson's old-fashioned ways, but it was difficult. This morning's lesson was about Moses and how his sister watched over him floating in the river. Miz Patterson's voice quivered with emotion as she related the story. Martha Ann and Molly tried not to look at each other. Miz Patterson always got excited about whatever story she was telling. Martha Ann rarely found anything to be excited about.

It's not that I'm not a Christian, Martha Ann thought. *I do believe in God and Jesus and all that. It's simply that these stories don't mean much today.* The story of Moses was no exception. Her thoughts continued to wander. She thought about the album she wanted to buy. She wanted to be able to go downtown again. She wanted everything to be normal, just the way it had always been.

CHAPTER EIGHT

Are children born with racial feelings? Or do they have to learn, first, what color they are and, second, what color is "best"?
    Kenneth B. Clark, *"How Children Learn About Race,"* Midcentury *White House Conference on Children and Youth*

May–August 1963
LETITIA

I've heard the expression "the days flew by" and it made me picture birds flying through the sky. But since the day of the fire hoses, now I picture birds swooping after a mean jay has tried to steal their eggs or something. That's how my days are flying by— full of anger. And hurt.

After that day with the fire hoses, I've been so torn. I am determined for the Movement to win, but I don't ever want to feel that water blasting me again. Mama and Daddy forbid me to go anyway, so I go on to school and come right home, but I don't want to give up on the Movement.

"Don't ever ask me to march again," Mae tells me one afternoon as we sit on my front porch. "I'll never forget those fire hoses."

"I know," I answer, "but we've got to be sure the Movement keeps going. Dr. King says we're almost to the point where we'll succeed. Yesterday some kids went and marched in their bathing suits, and remember the nonviolent training we got about how to curl up in a ball with our arms over our heads? We didn't do that."

"Don't ask me, Letitia. I mean it."

I know she does. I have to figure out another way to support the Movement. Maybe if I talk to Mama Lucy, I'll figure it out.

Mama and Daddy keep going down to the juvenile hall, trying to see Sam, but the police won't let anyone see their kids. Mama goes every day anyway, taking food, clean clothes, and notes. Etta and I make cards for Sam. Etta always draws stick figures of all our family at home again, all smiling. Mama doesn't know if Sam really gets the things she brings. I try to imagine what it's like for Sam, being locked up in one place, but I can't put my mind around it. At dinner, Mama can hardly eat anything. Etta keeps asking "when's Sammy coming home?" but no one knows how to answer her.

That night I slip into Mama Lucy's room before I go to bed. She's in bed, sitting up reading her Bible. She looks so small and frail against the pillows that I feel my breath catch for a moment. I curl up next to her, and she puts her arm 'round me.

"I don't know what to do about marching," I tell her. "I want to help make a difference, but I'm scared to ever march again. I can't stand to think of that water stabbing at me like it did. What should I do?"

"Now, sugar, you stay strong. There's hope now that things are gonna change. When I was a girl, 'twasn't so. There weren't no hope. Coloreds couldn't say out loud what was wrong and needed to change. Umhmm."

"So, should I disobey Mama and Daddy and march again?"

"Never disobey your folks." She shakes her head sternly. "The answer is right here in the Bible." She turns back pages and reads to me from Ecclesiastes. "'To everything there is a season, and a time to every purpose under heaven.' You see, sugar, this is the time for the Movement. You did your part in it. Now wait and watch for what your next part will be."

Talking to Mama Lucy helps. I guess I'll know what to do when it's time.

We hear lots of rumors at school. There were so many kids arrested every day that they filled up the jail and the juvenile hall.

They took kids to the Bessemer jail, and then to the fairgrounds, where they kept kids penned up where the livestock had been. Mae's cousin was kept there, and when she got home her mama said she smelled so bad she wanted to hose her off outside before she came in the house. But her cousin said, "Not a chance!" Someone said a few rich white people offered to keep kids locked in their fenced tennis courts, but I don't know if that's true.

Sam comes home from juvenile hall after twelve days.

"They're going to let you go back to school, son" is one of the first things Mama says to him after she hugs him close. "At first, the school board said they'd expel all the kids that marched, but there were so many, they couldn't do that." Mama shakes her head. I believe it would've broken her heart if Sam had been expelled.

"The teachers try not to show it, but we can tell they're glad we marched," I whisper to Sam as we slip into our places at the table.

At supper Mama can't stop watching him, and she keeps patting his arm, like she has to convince herself he's really home again.

"Tell us about it, son," Daddy urges. "How was you treated?"

Mama gets tears in her eyes. "Look at him, skinny as a rail."

"Ah, Mama. It weren't so bad. I think my whole class was together there. We sung a lot and hung out. I'm sure glad to be home though. We had baloney sandwiches on dry bread every day. I don't ever wanna see another baloney sandwich!"

"I heard some bad stuff about that Bessemer jail. They had this evil thing there called a steam box and they put some of the children in it. They say it had water on the floor, and when they crammed the children in there, it got so hot it were a wonder it didn't kill 'em."

"We didn't have nothing like that, Daddy. We did hear about them hosing everybody. Did you get hosed, Letitia?"

TURNER

I hang my head. It all comes back to me so real-like that I can't speak for the lump in my throat.

Sam's voice rushes on anyway, so he doesn't notice. "It was all worth it though. Rev. Bevel, he come and talk to us, and told us we won. These protests were for four things, he said, and we got all four."

"What four things?" pipes up Etta, her thick pigtails sticking out from her round, little head.

Sam puts down his fork and looks toward the ceiling as if the answer's written there. "Well, they wanted to integrate the lunch counters. That's one, and we got that, Rev. Bevel told us. Then they wanted the pools, golf courses, and all that kind of stuff to reopen after they closed them so they wouldn't have to integrate. That's s'posed to happen. Uh, they wanted to set up a group of Negroes and whites to work together on lots of the problems." He pauses. "Man, I forgot the other thing." He picks up his fork and shovels back into his mashed taters.

"They want the department stores to hire black clerks," I say softly. I'll never forget the four things 'cause we heard them so often at the mass meetings.

"Yeah, that's it," agrees Sam.

Etta looks at Sam, her eyes big like when she's surprised by something. "Did you and Lettie make the white people do all that?"

We have to laugh. Sometimes she says the funniest things. Daddy puts his arm 'round her. "Why, they sure did, honey. They was part of the protest with the great Dr. King, so they sure did make all that happen." When Daddy says that and looks at Sam and me, why, his expression is so full of pride it makes me feel good, and at this moment there isn't any room for anger and hurt. How could he have changed his mind so much? Would he let us be in the protest again?

That night, next to me in bed, Etta pushes off the sheet and curls closer 'round her stuffed rabbit. I turn the other way and try to get comfortable. The night's muggy, the warm, moist air like a blanket softly over us. I like hearing the sounds of Sam settling in bed too. Our house itself seems to sigh contentedly with everyone in their right place again.

I think I'll fall asleep quickly now that things are back to normal, but, instead, it seems like my mind is free so I find other things to worry about. My thoughts churn angrily inside my head. *Why do the whites want to keep us down so much? They don't even know us, and they think they're better than we are. If we do have to go to school with them, how will they treat us?*

Now that school's let out for the summer, I hang around the house a lot. Mae and I like to listen to the radio. Mae likes the fast songs best, but I'd rather hear the dreamy ones. Between us, though, we can spend hours listening to Shelley Stewart and Tall Paul White. The hot, humid air seeps into me and saps my energy. They talk about opening the pools and parks again. I hope that's true. Sometimes they open the fire hydrants so kids can splash around, but that reminds me too much of the fire hoses so I stay away. Mae and I walk down to Kelly Ingram Park once in a while, but it doesn't feel like our park anymore.

It's July, and Mama Lucy has to go to the hospital. She had a sore start on her foot, but no one noticed it until it was too late, and something bad got in her blood. I'm really scared for her 'cause Mama and Daddy look so worried. The hospital won't let kids in, so we can't visit her.

"Is she any better?" I ask when they get home from seeing her.

Daddy only shakes his head and goes in the other room. Mama says, "I don't think the doctors come on the colored floors very much. Although finally one did come while we was there." Mama got her mad face on. "He called Mama Lucy 'Auntie.' He say, 'Auntie, we're doing all we can, but you let this go on too long 'fore you came for help. Sorry.' Then he turned and left. Your daddy caught him in the hall. The doctor told him—" Mama stops as tears slide down her cheeks. "That doctor say there's not much hope."

I want to cover my ears and run away. What would we do without Mama Lucy? I can't bear to even think of it. Mama pulls me close, and I sob into her shoulder.

I go up to my room and sit on my bed holding the locket. That gift from Mama Lucy has come to mean even more to me. I feel like she's close to me when I can feel the solidness of that necklace.

When I think about the locket, I remember that morning of the march. The sky was gray, but there were these streaks of sunlight coming through, and I imagined they were little messages from God to encourage us, to say He was with us. Then there were those fire hoses like snakes, snakes full of prejudice and hate, and they were spewing that out at us. That's when the anger burns inside me. I remember that morning yelling "No!" But that force that Mama Lucy makes me feel from the locket changed that "No" to a "Yes!" Yes, I will be strong. Yes, I will never let anyone ever make me feel that humiliated or defeated again. Somehow, the feeling of "Yes!" is tied up in that locket. I'm so glad I found it again. Can it help me be strong about Mama Lucy now? I hope so.

Another week goes by with Mama Lucy still in the hospital. I come in from Mae's house and see Mama by the phone. She's standing there, holding the receiver against her chest, staring ahead.

"Mama," I say softly, "what is it?" although I know already. I know.

She turns as she hangs up the phone. "She's gone," she says as she reaches out to me. We hold each other as we weep, but the tears don't let the pain in my heart stop.

After the funeral, everyone comes back to our house. There's food spread out everywhere: fried chicken, casseroles, pickles, cakes, pies, everything. The buzz of noise from all the conversations gives me a headache. I slip away toward my room. As I start

upstairs I glance at Daddy. He looks so handsome in his dark
suit and crisp, white shirt, but his sad expression at the loss of
his mother breaks my heart even more. I dash to the safety of my
room.

I curl up on my bed, my hand clasping the locket I'm wearing. I thought I'd cried all the tears I could possibly have, but
more come. All I can do is call her name. "Mama Lucy. Mama
Lucy."

The summer simmers by. Every day I think about Mama Lucy
and miss her. Then I remember what she said: as long as someone's thinking of her, she lives on. I know she'll always be a part of
me.

They do open the pools and parks again, and Mae and I get
to enjoy them. One day, Mae and I are sipping sweet tea as we sit
on her porch listening to The Temptations. "Do you ever think
about when we marched for the Movement?" Mae asks.

"Oh, once in a while. It was something, wasn't it?"

She nods.

"I miss hearing Rev. Bevel and Dr. King and all of them."

As I think about those strong voices, I smile. I'll never forget the power of their message, their voices, gathering the whole
congregation together, bringing everyone to that point of being
united so that when Dr. King cried "are you with me?" there
could only be one answer: "Yes!"

I have come to love the power of Yes.

May–August 1963
MARTHA ANN

Martha Ann woke with a start. The knot in her stomach came
quickly as it always did when she heard her father's yelling. She
heard her mother crying "stop it, Harold! No, stop!" Martha Ann
folded her arms around her middle and tried to dig deeper under

the sheet. Her father's shouts continued, getting louder, more demanding.

Suddenly, her door flung open. Instead of Brad, her mother dashed in. Martha Ann sat up and gasped as she caught a glimpse of her mother, hair wild and loose around her tear-streaked face.

"It's nothing, sugar," her mother whispered breathlessly. "Go back to sleep. I think I'll just sit in here with you for a little while, that's all. Go to sleep."

"Mom," Martha Ann said, reaching for her mother. "What's going on? Are you OK?"

"Sure. Sure, I am." Her mother sat on the edge of the bed and stroked Martha Ann's hair as she held her close. "Your father's upset about our bills. It's better if I'm not right in front of him to yell at. It's OK."

Martha Ann began to cry. "What's happening, Mom? What's happening to us?"

Her mother shook her head, but there was no answer. She held Martha Ann for a few moments, then laid her down, rubbing her shoulder until Martha Ann slept again.

In the morning when Martha Ann came down for breakfast her father was already gone.

Her mother turned with a smile and set a plate of scrambled eggs on the table for Martha Ann. And Martha Ann wondered what was real anymore.

The summer dragged on. One afternoon, Molly suggested they go to the movies the next day. They took the bus downtown and walked the half block to the Alabama Theater. Martha Ann loved to go to the Alabama with its rich velvet curtain and the Wurlitzer organ rising out of the floor. Walking into the Alabama Theater was like walking into a palace. Every time she went, she was awed by the crystal chandeliers, the red and gold richness that surrounded her, and the amazing sound of the organ.

After the movie, *The Birds*, the girls were glad to get out into the bright sunlight.

"That was the scariest movie!" exclaimed Molly.

"We should have expected that from Alfred Hitchcock," said Martha Ann. "His movies are always so scary. I'm glad we didn't come see it at night."

Molly smiled and nodded. Both girls looked up into the blue, cloudless sky, as if assuring themselves that no birds were lurking nearby.

"You don't have to go home yet, do you?" Martha Ann asked. "I've been thinking about an éclair at Newberry's all afternoon."

The girls wandered over to Newberry's Department Store. Her mother had passed an extra dollar to Martha Ann, winking and saying "get yourself a special treat when you're in town." Martha Ann intended to do exactly that.

They slipped into some seats in the lunchroom, and Martha Ann picked up the menu, trying to decide the best treat to get. She loved the smell of Newberry's lunchroom, a sort of sugar and spice smell that promised delicious desserts: sundaes, éclairs, napoleons.

"Oh, my gosh," whispered Molly. "Look! I can't believe it."

Martha Ann looked in the direction Molly was nodding. Her mouth opened in surprise, and she felt a strange stirring of unease. A colored family was seated nearby, and they had actually been served. Martha Ann had never eaten in the same place as Negroes. She wondered what she should do. She wanted to stare at them, but she supposed she should simply ignore them. She didn't know where to look.

"Let's go," said Molly. "I don't want to eat in the same place they do." She started to gather up her purse.

Martha Ann's hand shot out and stopped her. "Wait. We can't just up and leave 'cause there's Negroes here."

Molly snorted as she raised her eyebrows. "Maybe you can't, but I sure can. My daddy would scold me something terrible if he knew I ate with coloreds."

Martha Ann increased her hold on her friend's arm. "You're

not eating with them. They're only in the same place. Come on, Molly. I want to get an éclair or something."

Molly's glance shot daggers at Martha Ann. "No, I'm leaving. You can come or not." She pulled her arm free and rose quickly.

Martha Ann sighed and rose too. *I guess my éclair will have to wait. Darn. Seems like the coloreds spoil things for me all the time.*

As the girls left, Martha Ann looked back at the colored family settled like an island in a sea of empty tables.

Summer moved along for Martha Ann. The swimming pools were open again, but now they were supposed to be integrated. At first, Martha Ann and her friends hesitated to go, but they soon learned that no Negroes would make their way over the mountain to their pool since it was for members only, so this summer didn't seem that different from any other.

Well, there were some differences, Martha Ann realized. She was growing taller, almost as tall as her mother. Finally, curves were developing on her body. She became more interested in how she looked. She spent hours studying the pictures of girls in *Seventeen* magazine, wanting to copy every new style. Often at night Martha Ann sat at her window in the dark, hoping for some soft breeze to cool her. She gazed out the window at her familiar neighborhood, at the moon, often glowing with a haze around it, breathing in the wonderful scent of confederate jasmine, and occasionally a tear would trickle from her eye. *Why does Daddy have to be like he is? We never know when we'll make him mad. I feel so alone sometimes. I don't want to tell Molly and Connie about Daddy. They've never seen him when he was mad. They might not even believe me. If they knew, they might not want to be friends with me. If the boys found out they might never ask me for a date. Why didn't Donald come talk to me at that last party?* Martha Ann looked up at the sky, the clouds dark gray outlined in silver. *Please, God, help me not to feel so lonely. I need to be thinking about what I'm going to do with my life, but I don't have any idea. Being sixteen's so hard!*

By August, Martha Ann was ready for vacation to be over. She, Molly, and Connie had become a threesome over the steamy summer. They went swimming as often as possible, their bodies smelling of chlorine long after they returned home. Sometimes they sat in the backyard, smearing baby oil and iodine over their slim arms and legs, hoping for that perfect tan.

Perspiration gathered on Martha Ann's upper lip before she declared, "I can't stand the heat anymore. Let's turn on the sprinkler." The girls took turns dashing through the cooling spray, shrieking and laughing as the water slapped gently against their skin. Martha Ann spun in a circle, dancing through the stream of water, and the droplets caught the sun's rays, becoming a string of crystals before her eyes. *How beautiful*, she thought.

They collapsed back on their towels and let the sun bake them dry again.

"I can hardly wait for school to start," said Molly.

"Me too," agreed Connie. "My mom says these last years of high school are going to fly by. I surely hope not."

Martha Ann nodded. "I'm in no hurry. I don't know what I want to do after high school.

"I know exactly," said Connie. "I'm going to Auburn and then become a teacher, then I'm going to marry someone, maybe a doctor, and come back here and live the rest of my life right here."

Molly looked pensive. "I don't know what I want to be, but I want to get married and have a family. Maybe I'll be a secretary or something."

Martha Ann smiled at her friends. "My mom wants me to go to college. She says that in this day and age a girl needs to get a college education. She says there are good jobs for women, and we need to be able to take care of ourselves."

"Yeah, this is the age of women's liberation."

"What does that mean anyway?" asked Molly. "I've read

about women burning their bras, but I'm not about to do that."

Connie shook her head. "No, that's not what it's about. My mom told me all about it. It's about women having more choices, having careers if we want them. We could be doctors, ourselves, or lawyers, or anything."

"Well, then who's going to stay home and take care of the kids and the house and all that stuff?" asked Martha Ann.

Shrugging, Connie said, "I dunno. Maybe the husbands?"

The three girls fell back on their towels, laughing at the idea.

Summer days moved along on both sides of the mountain: for some, pushed by the warmth of the sun's heat, for others, pushed by the heat of determination for a new day.

CHAPTER NINE

A racist is someone who despises someone because of his color, and
an Alabama segregationist is one who conscientiously believes that it is in
the best interests of Negroes and whites to have separate education
and social order.
    Gov. George C. Wallace, *U.S. News and World Report, 1964*

Early September 1963
LETITIA

By the end of summer I feel a restlessness for that feeling of
striving for something that I get at school. The whole experience
of the Movement makes me sure I want to be a teacher. Mama
always tells us that education is the way to get what we need. Now
I really believe her, and I want to be part of that for all Negroes.
Besides, I really miss Mama Lucy when I'm home. I keep expecting her to come in from her room and sit at the table with us.
Maybe at school I won't be thinking about her so much.

There is a lot of talk that Birmingham schools will finally
be integrated. The word is that it will involve only three white
schools—Graymont Elementary, and West End and Ramsay High
Schools—and only five Negro kids will be moved to those schools.
Two Negroes were admitted to the University of Alabama in spite
of Gov. Wallace's stand against it. The federal government is looking at racial issues for some legislation, and Dr. King led a huge
March on Washington, so things are happening. It can be dangerous, though, as we learned yet again, when Medgar Evers, the
Negro civil rights leader, was shot right in front of his house. After
we heard that news I couldn't sleep. Mama cried most of the night.

TURNER

All the progress makes me excited but I can't help but be a little bit afraid for when school opens on September 4.

Finally, the first day of school, my sophomore year. I dress carefully in my blue jumper and cream-colored blouse. Listening to Shelley Stewart on the radio, I just have to laugh. Even when he talks about an important subject, he talks so wild and crazy that we can't be serious. I wish it was a bright, sunny day, but the clouds hang low and gray over the city.

Mama is ready for us downstairs with breakfast and instructions. "Now, y'all eat all your breakfast 'fore you go. I don't want any of my children going to school hungry, hear?" Mama says as she gives us one of her stern looks.

"Ah, Mama," Sam mutters as he jumps up, leaving half a bowl of cereal but grabbing his toast. He kisses her good-bye and dashes out the door.

"Well, y'all finish up," she says to Etta and me. She spreads out the paper in front of her, studying the grocery ads. "Ham, 45 cents a pound; sugar, 9 cents for 5 pounds; pound package of Quaker Oats grits, 10 cents," she murmurs to herself. Turning the page, she exclaims, "Well, look at this. 'Dr. and Miz A. G. Gaston to be White House guests.' Well, imagine that. Our own folk, going to dinner at the White House."

"How come?" I ask.

"'Cause they rich, I reckon. Says they'll be at a state dinner for the king and queen of Af . . ." Mama peers closer at the word as she sounds it out. "Afghanistan. Mmm hmm, imagine that."

Etta waves her cereal spoon in the air. "I wanna go too. I wanna eat with a king and queen."

Mama laughs and kisses the top of Etta's head. "I don't think so, sugar." I smile at her as I gather up my things for school.

Mae and I fall into step at the corner as we usually do. It feels so good to be starting school again. The two boys who are walking ahead of us, Damon and Raphael, slow and join us. I notice they both have grown taller during the summer, and now

Damon is half-a-head taller than me. I let myself imagine dancing with him at the first school dance and smile up at him. This is
gonna be a good year, I can feel it. At Parker High School we pass
through the gateway of the chain-link fence. I wonder how many
of the other kids are remembering that historic day last May. I
certainly am.

Mr. Johnson, dressed in a dark suit and neat white shirt,
stands in the doorway welcoming all of us. His round glasses on
his round face make him look owlish, wise.

"Morning, Mr. Johnson," I say as I pass him, and he nods
back at me. He has such a strong, sturdy look, I can't imagine how
we all had the courage to ignore his authority and leave school
that day. After all, our ministers, the principal, any adults are to
be obeyed. That's the way it is. I shake my head in wonder and
walk to my new homeroom.

Kids are still talking about the marches, but not what we all
went through: jails, the hosing, the dogs. They are talking about
the difference we made. Almost everyone went swimming in
some pool during the summer, and most had gone downtown to
sit at the lunch counters and get served. I still haven't tried that.
Mama says she's going to take Sam, Etta, and me real soon.

The school day rushes by too quickly. Mae and I walk home
slowly, comparing classes. When I get home, Mama's already
heard about what happened at the schools they tried to integrate.
I don't know how Mama does it, but she knows everything that's
going on in our community as soon as it happens.

"Did any white folks bother y'all today?" she asks as soon as
I walk in the door.

"No, Mama. Nobody bothered us at all."

"Well, I'm just glad you don't go to West End. They had
white demonstrators walking around the school with signs saying
bad things. 'Course, they had the police there to stop any trouble."
Mama makes that expression of hers when she doesn't believe
something. I have to smile.

"What about the other schools?" I ask.

"Same thing. Maybe that rain kept people home. At the elementary school only a few of the white students showed up. They're afraid some of our black might rub off on them."

That makes me want to giggle, but I can tell Mama is provoked. Really, it makes me mad too, but it's what we expect.

Mama sighs, "Well, leastwise there weren't no riots. I'm just thankful for that. Now, tell me about your classes, sugar."

That night I am deep in a dream when I hear the telephone ring. A call that late at night can mean only bad news. Etta sleeps through it, but Sam and I slip out of bed and go to see what happened. Daddy is hanging up the phone and shaking his head.

"What is it?" Mama asks, her voice full of concern.

Daddy sees us and opens his arms. We run to him and he holds us close.

"They bombed Arthur Shores' house again. They's a big riot going on down there by Dynamite Hill. People getting shot. It's a bad business."

I know who Arthur Shores is—an important Negro lawyer. Back when that Autherine Lucy wanted to get into the university, it was Mr. Shores that was her lawyer. And Dynamite Hill's not the real name, but people call it that 'cause there's been so many bombings over there.

We all sit down in the living room. "Because of the schools?" Mama asks.

Daddy shrugs. "I s'pose. Do they really need a reason?"

We all sit there in the dim light, both with our silent thoughts. I wonder what Mama Lucy would say. She lived through lots a' things like bombings and lynchings and such. I remember her saying *don't let the hard things those ignorant and mean white folks do turn your heart to stone; the Lord'll take care of all a' them in the by-an'-by.* I reach my hand up to hold my locket. I even wear it when I go to bed now.

Finally, Mama sighs a deep sigh. "There's not a thing we can do about it. Let's get back to bed."

We all rise, hug each other, and go on, the heaviness of the message weighing hard on our shoulders. Tomorrow we'll learn if any friends have been hurt.

When I slip into bed, Etta stirs awake. "What's a matter?" she asks sleepily.

"Another bombing," I tell her, then regret my words. Five-year-olds don't need to know about such things. They'll learn soon enough. I hug her until she goes back to sleep.

The next day when Mama gets home from working over the mountain at the Pierce's house, she's carrying a big paper sack.

"Look, sugar," she says, sitting down on my bed with the sack at her feet. "Miz Pierce give me some real pretty clothes for you that her girl outgrowed. Come look." She smiles at me as she starts to pull out the dresses. The first one she pulls out is that sailor dress I saw at the birthday party, the party where I had to be washing dishes in the kitchen.

Seeing it makes me mad. "Mama, I don't need any hand-me-downs from some white girl. Giving things to us only makes them feel like they're better than we are. I don't want any part a' that." I turn my back.

"Now, looka here, girl, don't you be so uppity yourself." Mama's voice has that steely edge to it that makes me turn around and face her. "Who you think you are that you're too big to accept a gift, hmm? I grew up wearing hand-me-downs, and it didn't bother me none. You've always been glad to get those hand-me-downs before. Miz Pierce was being nice. It won't hurt you to wear these dresses. That little missy of hers and her white friends won't never see you, so what do you care?"

"Well, look at this one, Mama." I hold up a skirt that has the hem torn. "She's giving us the old rags she's too lazy to throw away."

"That's enough, Letitia. You got no reason to be disrespectful. You stop that now."

I know Mama's right, but I can't help how I feel. After I felt that beating down by the fire hoses and realized how much

83

whites don't like us, I can hardly stand to have anything to do with anything white, and that's the truth, no matter what I think Mama Lucy would whisper in my ear.

Early September 1963
MARTHA ANN

One evening a few days before school started Martha Ann curled up on the couch with her dad as he watched *Hawaiian Eye*. Brad sat on the floor building a cardboard-box garage for one of his Matchbox cars. Recently, there hadn't been any late-night outburst from her father, and Martha Ann was hopeful that her parents were working things out.

During a commercial break Mr. Pierce turned to Martha Ann. "I was afraid I was gonna have to pull you kids outta school this fall. They're talking about integrating for sure, but today I heard it's not gonna be your school."

Brad looked up for a moment, then immediately seemed to lose interest in the conversation.

Martha Ann bolted up straight. "But what would we do if we didn't go to school?" she asked, alarm sounding in her voice.

"Oh, you'd still go to school, just not one with niggers in it. I've heard about these academies starting up that would be for whites only."

"Daddy, I want to go to school with my friends, the same school I've always gone to."

"Keep your shirt on, sugar. There's nothing to worry about. I told you, they're not gonna integrate your school."

"But what if they do someday? I don't want to change schools. You have to let me stay with my friends."

Mr. Pierce slapped his hand down on the couch and Martha Ann jumped. "Now, you listen to me, little miss. You're gonna do what I tell you as long as you're under my roof. I'm not gonna have my kids going to school with no niggers, hear? End of discussion." He turned back to the TV.

Martha Ann hunched down farther in the cushions. She looked up and saw her mother watching her from the wing chair. Her mother's steady gaze and her hand raised slightly as if she were patting her daughter's arm let Martha Ann know in that special mother-daughter unspoken language that she should settle down, not worry. An almost-smile flitted across Martha Ann's face as she, too, turned back to *Hawaiian Eye*. In spite of her father's outburst there hadn't been the terrible anger that might have come. That was something, anyway, maybe a good sign for the future.

Sitting in bed that night, Martha Ann finished writing in her diary and began to think about what her dad had told her. *What if the coloreds do come to my school? No one will speak to them or sit by them. I'm sure we won't talk or anything. What happens if a teacher makes us work on a project with them? How could we do that?* She tried to picture having coloreds sitting in a desk next to her, trying to share a book or subject notes, but she simply couldn't bring an image to mind.

I know they've passed a law saying we have to integrate. When that happens, what should I do? I know Jesus would tell me to be friendly to them. What if I'm nice to them, but they're mean back to me?

Questions without answers twisted through her mind. *Why can't things stay the same?* Even though her school would not be involved in the new integration, Martha Ann couldn't help but have some fears about what might happen when school opened on September 4.

The next evening, Mr. Pierce kicked the door shut behind him when he got home after work. Waving the rolled-up paper in front of him, he chortled, "Well, those nig—, I mean Negroes"— the word slurred as he dragged it out—"those Negroes didn't do very well with their integrating."

Martha Ann's mother scowled. "Did you stop somewhere

on your way home, Harold?"

"Just a little celebration drink at the club, that's all. They think they can do anything they want, but now they got another think coming. There was another little explosion over at Dynamite Hill last night, and today the superintendent of the schools, he closed those schools so's no Neee-groes"—the word stretched out again—"can come in."

Martha Ann looked up from setting the table. "Daddy, why are you so against the coloreds?"

"Why? I'll tell you why, little lady. 'Cause they aren't like us. They don't know how to think like we do. They are dirty and don't take baths. They smell bad, and they carry diseases. They take jobs away from whites at the mills. Their menfolk are full of lust."

"Harold!" Mrs. Pierce interrupted. "Watch what you say in front of the children. Now, let's sit down and eat. I've been keeping supper warm waiting on you."

"I'm just answering my daughter." He pulled out his chair and sat down, as they all gathered at the table. "And one last thing. God didn't mean for the races to be together. Have you ever seen a blackbird and a robin mate? No. It's against God's law."

"Harold. Enough," Mrs. Pierce said as she dished some brisket onto her plate and passed the serving dish.

Martha Ann looked at her dad. *Are all those things he said true?*

"Martha Ann." Her mother startled her from her thoughts. "Pass the slaw."

The next morning as Martha Ann got ready to leave for school, her mother stopped her at the door.

"Now, darlin', if they close your school, you come right home. If there's any trouble, you stay away from it."

"Oh, Mom, don't worry. There's not going to be any trouble here. They won't come over the mountain."

"I hope not," she said, shaking her head. "I heard that Huntsville integrated their schools without any problems. I don't see why we can't do the same," she muttered, heading back to the kitchen.

Martha Ann had spent so much of last May worrying about the Negroes bringing their violence over the mountain, but nothing had happened. She wasn't about to spoil the new school year fretting about something that probably never would occur. She, Molly, and Connie had spent all last Saturday talking about this sophomore year they were starting.

"I'm not going to worry about Sandra and Karen and all of them," declared Connie. "I'm going to be my own person, like my mom is always telling me to be."

"Well, I'm going to be nice to everyone," said Molly.

"I'm going to keep up with all my schoolwork" was Martha Ann's affirmation.

The three friends looked at each other and burst out laughing.

"Let's face it," said Connie. "We'll be the same as we always are."

Martha Ann nodded. "Except, I don't think I care as much about Donald this year."

"Who, then?"

"I don't know. Maybe Tommy."

The three munched cookies and spent the rest of the afternoon planning what to wear on the first day of school.

Their conversation turned to whether or not Miss Alabama, Judy Short, would win the Miss America contest next weekend in Atlantic City and how Joe Namath would do in Saturday's game at the University of Alabama—everyday things, the things that make up our steps through life. Martha Ann's thoughts, however, kept returning to her parents. Would things be better or would her father's temper get more violent?

CHAPTER TEN

Adversity is like a strong wind. It tears away from us all but the things that cannot be torn, so that we see ourselves as we really are.
Arthur Golden, *Memoirs of a Geisha*

September 15, 1963
LETITIA

Fall is my favorite time of year. Mama Lucy always said it's a season full of promise. I like it 'cause it's the start of a new school year, a new class at Sunday school, school parties and dances all ahead of us. Fall is so full of excitement and looking forward to things. It's sort of like when we have a snowfall here in Alabama—it's so beautiful for the moment, even if it's soon gone or left muddy and soot-stained. But for that moment as the first flakes fall and we run outside to catch them on our tongues, oh, I love the happy way it makes me feel.

Mae and I have a few classes together, and I like all my teachers and subjects, 'though I am a little worried about algebra. Damon's in my class, and he's real good at math and said he'd help me if I needed it. I think Mae's a little jealous about that. There's a new boy this year, Lewis, from Mississippi. He's on the football team, and he seems nice. He's really cute. He talked to me in homeroom yesterday.

On Saturday, Mae and I walk down to Kelly Ingram Park. The more time passes from that terrible day of the hosing, the more I feel like this is our park again. Even though I still get angry thinking about the way whites treat Negroes, I'm not quite as mad as I was. It's like Mama Lucy has been talking to me all

TURNER

summer, kinda calming me down.

This morning as I get ready for church, I stand in front of the full-length mirror on the bathroom door. I'm wearing my hair a little longer, and I like it this way. I smile thinking what my parents would say if I grew it into an Afro like so many of the boys are doing, and even some of the girls. My dress is a soft rose color with a white collar, and I have on my new black shoes with the little heels. I like my reflection that looks more like a teenager than a girl.

Our family always gets to church early so Mama and Daddy can visit with all their friends. 'Course, that suits us kids too. We've been going to St. John's A.M.E. Church all my life. It's where Mama Lucy went too. I like our preacher, Rev. C. E. Thomas, but what I like most about church is the youth activities and the singing. After going to the mass meetings at the different churches, I have to say I like St. John's the best. 'Course, Sixteenth Street Baptist is the biggest 'cause that's where all the rich people go, and it will always be special to me 'cause of the Movement, but I love St. John's the most. Between Sunday school and church at 11:00, we kids always hang out together in the halls or sometimes outside if the weather's OK. So we're watching the clock, waiting for Sunday school to be over so's we can laugh and talk together. All of a sudden, there's a huge rumble. I swear I feel the earth shake. It's a cloudy day, but the sound isn't like any thunder I've ever heard.

"What is that?" several cry.

"Is it an earthquake?"

We grab at each other and look around. The shaking stops, and we rush outside.

"Look! Over there," someone shouts. Everyone's pouring out of the church. A hum of voices becomes a throbbing noise as everyone's talking, asking what's going on. As we look around, a huge cloud of gray smoke billows from a block to the southeast.

"It's the Sixteenth Street Church" I hear someone yell. Ev-

90

eryone takes off running in that direction.

"A bomb. Was it a bomb? Oh, my God, have they bombed the church?" the buzz of voices sizzles along as we all race in that direction.

We can hear the sirens of the fire trucks as we get near the church. The police cars are pulling up, the officers yelling at everyone as they jump out of their cars.

"Get back, everyone! Stop crowding and let the fire trucks get in," they keep shouting, but people aren't paying them much mind. Everyone from that church has run outside, and people are coming from every direction.

"What is it? What happened?" everyone's asking. The smoke smells so strong and burns our eyes. I see a man with blood dripping down his face. People are crying, children yelling "Mama," "Daddy," some shouting out names as they hurry to find people in their families. The smoke and dust fill the air around us like a cloak of something evil. Mama, Daddy, and Etta come up to where I'm standing. My heart is racing, my breath coming in quick gasps. I feel so frightened. Mama puts her hand on my shoulder. I can feel her trembling, or maybe it's me.

"It was a bomb." That hateful word jumps from mouth to mouth through the mass of people, and I feel the same anger that is building all around me. The police are coming through all of us, trying to get us to break up. The preacher of the church, Rev. Cross, is on the front steps shouting something into one of those bullhorns. This is all so different from when we were marching out those same doors with the Movement. There is no sense of hopeful excitement and good feelings here now. There's only anger. And fear.

"The Lord is my Shepherd. I shall not want. Yea, though . . ." I know the Twenty-third Psalm that Rev. Cross shouts into the megaphone, but I can't pray it with him. No one can.

"Come on," says Daddy. "There's gonna be trouble here. I want my family safe." He looks at me so sternly, I have to follow him and Mama and Etta.

I look around quickly and ask, "Where's Sam?"

Daddy stops. "Y'all go on back to our church. I'll get Sam and meet you there. Go on, now."

Mama picks up Etta, and we push our way through the crowd.

Shots blast out, and we look back quickly.

"Just the police shooting warning shots," Mama determines, so we turn and head to St. John's. When we get there, Rev. Thomas is urging everyone inside to pray, and we join them. I can't pray though. I have such a knot in my stomach, I almost feel sick. I keep seeing that pile of bricks, the smoke, the scraps of curtains hanging limp in the trees along the street like dead flags of hope destroyed.

It seems like forever until Daddy and Sam come. I look up to see them walking toward us, and for a second my heart stops beating when I see tears in Daddy's eyes. He walks to Rev. Thomas and whispers in his ear as Sam slips in beside me.

"They kilt some people," says Sam softly to me.

Killed? Oh, God, no! We've had bombings before, but no one has ever been killed.

Rev. Thomas makes the announcement, and our cries and sobs lift like a big bird flying to heaven, going to God because there is no other place to go. But I find no comfort here. I wonder who's been killed. How will their families find out? What will they do then? What can they do?

After Daddy sits in prayer for a few minutes, he takes Mama's hand and says, "Let's go home." Mama nods. Etta's crying softly, huddled in Mama's lap. Sam and I look at each other, and in our silent glances we share our grief, but also our anger.

Even though it's only mid-afternoon when we get home, I go to my room and lie down on my bed. I don't have any words for what I'm feeling. My body aches with a sadness deeper than anything I've ever known.

We don't learn the names of the girls until late that afternoon. Someone called Mama and told her. She comes slowly into my room and sits on the edge of my bed. Her hand strokes my back, back and forth, back and forth.

"Baby," she begins. "Baby, these are the girls. Addie Mae Collins, Denise McNair, Cynthia Wesley, and Carole Robertson. Did you know any of them?" I can hear the grief in her voice, the way her breath catches in her throat.

I lie still, curled up on my side. I feel like I've been kicked in my stomach and all the air had gone out of me. Carole goes— went—to Parker and was in the marching band. She was one of the best students. We weren't friends the way Mae and I are or any of the girls that I sit with at lunch, but I knew her. I knew her, and now she is dead. How can someone my age be dead from a bomb? A bomb at church! I feel so numb I can't even cry.

Mama tries to sit me up, to put her arms around me. I'm so cold I have goose bumps on my arms. She hugs me to her and rocks back and forth. I wish I was as small as Etta so I could climb in her lap. But even Mama can't kiss away this hurt. I try to say something, to tell her I knew Carole, but the lump in my throat is so big I can't get the words out. I start to cry then, to sob and wail. I beat my fists against her arms. I cry so hard my eyes ache and my head hurts. I've lost the power of "Yes" and I can only say "No." I say it over and over. "No! No!" But it doesn't do any good. This terrible thing has happened, and it never can be undone. My grief is too big. The sadness is for Carole and the others, for their families, for our schools. It's for our churches that will never feel safe again. It's for our neighborhoods that have lost children who can never play in them again. And it's for our world that will never be the same. Safe, will we ever feel safe? If our churches aren't safe, no place can ever be.

I can't hold in all this sadness. I cry and cry. Mama doesn't say a word, only holds me close. She's crying too. How can we go on from this point, where girls like me are killed at church? I don't see any answer. Even Mama Lucy can't help me.

September 15, 1963
MARTHA ANN

As usual, Mrs. Pierce hurried the family off to church. Martha Ann didn't mind because she was wearing her new shoes with the two-inch heels, and she couldn't wait to show them off to the other girls at Sunday school. She had worried that her father would say something, but he didn't even seem to notice. She had wanted these shoes ever since she first had seen them at Sears, and finally her mother had consented to buy them. Martha Ann was beginning to feel like a teenager instead of a girl, and she liked the feeling. She couldn't help but notice that she was a tiny fraction of an inch taller than her mother now.

At church, Martha Ann rushed to her Sunday school room and was glad to see Sandra, Molly, and a few others already there. As the lesson began, Martha Ann's mind began to wander. *Poor Miz Patterson. She tries so hard to keep our attention, but it never quite works for her. It doesn't help that with this lesson about our loving one another, Molly whispered to me "does that mean Donald or Tommy?"* It was sure hard for us not to giggle out loud. After the church service ended at noon, the family drove home to their big Sunday dinner. Mrs. Pierce had put a roast and potatoes in the oven before she left. Now back home, she scurried around making gravy, heating the canned green beans, and putting her yeast rolls in the oven. Martha Ann's job was to set the table. As she did so she wondered why Brad and her dad didn't have some chore to do too.

Soon after they sat down at the table, the phone rang, and Mrs. Pierce jumped up to answer it. She quickly covered the few steps to the wall phone hanging by the kitchen door.

"Yes" they could hear her saying over and over.

"Oh, no!" she cried out, causing the family to look her way and listen. After she hung up the phone, she slowly walked to the table.

"What's that about?" asked Mr. Pierce, pausing with his

fork midway to his mouth.

Martha Ann noticed the strange expression on her mother's face, and she felt that knot of fear in her stomach that told her to be ready for bad news.

"That was Cynthia Willard. There's been a bombing."

"A bombing?" exclaimed Brad.

Mrs. Pierce put a shaky hand on the back of her chair, then sat down, staring ahead.

"Well?" said Mr. Pierce, gesturing for her to continue.

"A bomb. At that Negro church that was the gathering place for all those marchers."

"Ha!" saidMr. Pierce loudly, a tiny splat of potatoes spraying onto his plate. "Serves them right."

Mrs. Pierce looked up at her husband, her expression cold and angry. "What a terrible thing to say, Harold. There were four girls killed."

Martha Ann gasped. Even Brad looked startled.

"Four girls about the age of Martha Ann. How would you feel if it was your daughter?"

Martha Ann's father gave his daughter a quick glance, then looked back at his wife. "Well, it's too bad about those girls, but it's the niggers' own fault. They're always causing some kinda trouble."

"Causing trouble? And what kind of trouble is bad enough to turn around and kill children? Can you tell me that? And in church too!" Mrs. Pierce's face was flushed and her eyes flashed with anger. Martha Ann and Brad looked silently from one parent to the other. Martha Ann couldn't remember her mother ever standing up to her father so strongly.

When her father responded his voice was icy hard, and anger glittered in his eyes. "That's enough, Lily. I work hard for this family, and I expect to be able to sit through a nice Sunday dinner without my wife carrying on about some niggers."

Mrs. Pierce let out a big breath of air as her shoulders slumped down, and Martha Ann could see the spirit go out of her mother like a balloon deflating. Mrs. Pierce looked down at her plate and slowly began eating again. Her father glared at his wife for a long moment, then began shoveling food back in his mouth. Not another word was spoken the entire rest of the meal.

That evening the family sat in the living room and watched the news, as usual. The lead story was about the bombing at the Sixteenth Street Baptist Church. Martha Ann watched as the television cameras zoomed in on the gaping hole in the side of the church building. Piles of bricks lay in heaps. Soon the black-and-white screen showed pictures of the four girls who had been killed, and the reporter read their names: Addie Mae Collins, Denise McNair, Carole Robertson, and Cynthia Wesley. A litany of heartbreak. Martha Ann glanced at her mother and saw tears trickling down her cheeks. Her father sat in grim silence seeming to hold his breath until the news story ended, as if the report had a bad smell. Brad shifted uncomfortably next to Martha Ann.

Martha Ann felt like weeping herself. She couldn't imagine what it must have been like for those girls to die that way. She thought how horrible it would be if Molly or Connie or anyone she knew would be killed by a bomb blast, how terrible she would feel. *And they were only at church. How can a church not be a safe place?* It was more than she could take in.

When she got ready for bed that night her thoughts kept returning to the deaths of those four girls. She laid out her skirt and blouse for the next day and brushed her hair. She couldn't help thinking that in Birmingham there were four girls that could never be doing that again.

The night sounds of the house settled around her. She plumped her pillow and snuggled into her usual comfortable position. *Those poor girls and their families and friends. I feel like I should do something.* And so she prayed. *Dear Jesus, please be with those families and comfort them. Amen.* Then she turned over and fell asleep.

CHAPTER ELEVEN

*The death of these little children may lead our whole Southland
from the low road of man's inhumanity to man to the high road of peace
and brotherhood. . . . The spilled blood of these innocent girls may cause
the whole citizenry of Birmingham to transform the negative extremes of
a dark past into the positive extremes of a bright future. Indeed, this tragic
event may cause the white South to come to terms with its conscience.*

Dr. Martin Luther King, Jr., *Eulogy for Addie May Collins, Denise
McNair, and Cynthia Wesley, September 19, 1963*

September 16–18, 1963
LETITIA

Sam comes in and sits by me on my bed. After a moment he says
quietly, "Some of the guys wanna go bomb a white church, make
them see how it feels."

I look at him quickly. "Oh, no, Sam. That would only make
things worse. Did you talk to them, try to stop them?"

"Yeah. I don't think they'll go. But we all feel like we wanna
fight back. We can't help it."

I nod. "I know. I feel the same way too. We can't fight back,
though, because we can never win. But I can't be like our ministers who are saying we should pray for the whites and forgive
them."

When I try to fall asleep, I can't even though I feel exhaust-
ed. This anger is getting so strong inside me, it's becoming all of
me. I feel it fill me up, like when I fill a glass with water. It seeps
up through my whole body, into my legs and arms, and the force
of it makes my legs want to run fast—away—and my hands curl

into fists and my arms want to hit back.

But I can't do that. I can't do anything.

I don't see how I can go to school today, after what happened
yesterday, but Mama makes me. She says we owe it to Carole to
go on with life. Mae and I walk to school together, but after our
first few words, we walk in silence. As we get to Parker, everyone
seems to be speaking softly. Mr. Johnson stands by the door and
looks as if he wept all night. We might have a special assembly or
something, but we don't. Our teachers don't say anything about
the bombing; we kids don't talk about it. Like we can't even speak
of such a terrible thing. But it's there, all around us, like a sad,
gray mist.

Carole's funeral is on Tuesday afternoon, and everyone
from school goes. The service is held at my church, St. John's. Tomorrow there will be services for the other three at Sixth Avenue
Baptist. They say that Dr. King will speak there. But today, Rev.
Shuttlesworth does Carole's service along with Rev. Cross from
her church. I can't look at her family. It hurts too much to see
how sad they are.

Mae and I sit on our front steps afterward. "I keep thinking
about the Movement. Did all this violence happen because of the
Movement, or would it have happened anyway?" Mae asks me.

I shrug. "But we have to have the Movement. Daddy heard
that there have been nearly fifty bombings of Negroes in the last
twenty years. The ministers all are preaching to forgive these
people and to pray for them. I can't do that. I'm so angry. I don't
want to turn around and hurt white people because of this, but
I sure don't want to have anything to do with them. I wish we
could keep them out of our world, like they try to keep us out of
theirs."

"Oh, Letitia—" she begins, but I cut her off.

"Sometimes, though, I wonder what the Movement is for.
I don't want to be discriminated against, but I want to stay safe
over here. Daddy wants us to be secure in our home, and Mama

wants us to trust in the Lord and love everybody. I wish I could talk to Mama Lucy. I wish we hadn't been hosed. I wish . . ." Tears start to pool in my eyes. "I wish so many things."

Mae looks at me quietly for a moment. "I feel that way too." "The whole country and the government are paying some attention, our leaders say. If we stop we might lose everything we've worked for. Things can change, can't they? We can't give up now." I want to believe that. I want all these bad things to count toward something good. I shake my head. But in my mind, I can't hear any words of strength from Mama Lucy.

All the anger and sadness makes me feel so tired. My body can't relax, like it wants to get up and do something, fight or scream or wail. I think I'll have trouble falling asleep, but I must have been in a deep sleep because the sound of crying simply seeps into my dream and doesn't startle me awake. Finally, I realize the crying isn't part of my dream.

"Etta, what is it? What's the matter?"

Etta tucks her little body close to me and puts her arms around my neck.

"Were you having a bad dream?" I ask her, pulling her even closer.

I feel her nod against my shoulder.

"Don't cry. No monsters can get you."

"Not monsters," she sniffles, "bad men."

"Bad men?"

"Mmmhmm. I was swinging on the gate. A big car drove by and the bad mens were in it."

"Oh, Etta, there's no bad men around here," I tell her. I pat her back for a minute.

"But there is. There is bad mens. They threw bombs at me. And I couldn't run away 'cause I was swinging on the gate."

I feel a catch in my throat and I can't speak for a moment. Because it's true. We know that now from the bombing at the church. There are bad men who will come to our safe places. They will throw bombs. And we can't get away. What can I say to my little sister?

Nothing.

I just hold her close.

September 16, 1963
MARTHA ANN

Martha Ann walked into school the next day expecting all the talk to be about the bombing. She was surprised to find that nothing was different at school that morning. Chatter before the first bell was as loud as always, laughter rang out from different little groups in the hall, boys elbowed and shoved each other, girls whispered together.

She was glad to see Connie and Molly already in their homeroom. She put her books down on her desk and walked to where they were standing. "Isn't it awful about those girls being killed?"

Molly and Connie both nodded, and Connie said, "My daddy told me this morning that two Negro boys were shot and killed too."

"What?" exclaimed Martha Ann. "Shot at the church?"

"No. One boy was riding his bike, and some white boys drove by and shot him. The other was shot by a policeman. He'd thrown a brick or something."

Molly moved away to talk to Sandra, and Connie and Martha Ann simply shook their heads and looked out the window. There were no words for the terrible things that had happened.

Martha Ann moved through the morning still expecting something to be said, but nothing was. After going through the lunch line, she carried her tray to the usual place. At the lunch table the conversation revolved around what everyone had done over the weekend. To Martha Ann the talk was like ribbons swirling, things of no substance connected to nothing.

Connie broke into the conversation. "Don't you all know about the bombing of that Negro church, about those girls that were killed?"

"'Course we know," Sandra said as she turned her back toward Connie and whispered to the girl next to her.

"But don't you care?"

Sandra turned slowly back and stared a long moment at Connie, a look of complete disdain on her face. "Why should we care? It doesn't have anything to do with us."

Martha Ann began to feel uneasy. Connie was a friend of hers, but this was obviously not something she should be talking about. She should drop the subject. *Why is she doing this? Everyone's going to snub her from now on if she's not careful.*

Connie wiped her mouth. She didn't seem to be aware of the icy chill that had descended on the group. She leaned toward Sandra as if they were talking about any old subject.

"But it does. It does have something to do with us. They were girls about our age, just going to church. And they were killed by a bomb because some white people don't like Negroes."

"So?" Sandra's eyes had narrowed, her jaw clenched.

"So they're human beings, the same as we are. That shouldn't have happened."

A hush fell over everyone at the table as they looked from Connie to Sandra. The other girls shrank back.

Sandra looked around the table, then back at Connie. "You're showing your ignorance. They are not like us, and everyone knows it. You've become a nigger-lover, Connie, and you ought to be ashamed."

Martha Ann gasped at the insult, but Connie looked Sandra straight in the eye. "I'm not. I don't even know any Negroes. I just don't think innocent people should be killed because whites don't want to mix with Negroes."

"If you're not a nigger-lover then why are you talking about them all the time? Face it, we don't care. Maybe you'd better find another table to sit at for lunch." Sandra threw her paper napkin on top of her tray. "Come on, girls, let's go." She stood up and let her glance swing around to all sitting there. There was no doubt that an implicit order was in that look. The other girls looked quickly at each other, then got up too.

Sandra's gaze fell on Martha Ann, who sat scarcely breathing, unable to move. "And you're probably one too, Martha Ann Pierce." With that, like a queen followed by her ladies-in-waiting, Sandra and her friends swept down the aisle. Other tables of students, so engrossed in their own conversations, didn't seem to notice the dramatic moment, but Martha Ann felt a chilling emptiness surround her.

She sat staring straight ahead, her eyes burning with tears as she tried to keep them from falling. The lump in her throat made any words impossible. She felt stunned. She had no intention of standing up for the Negroes, but how could she leave Connie stranded all alone? *Why did she have to bring this up?* Resentment for putting her in a bad position rose up in Martha Ann. She glared at Connie, who was calmly finishing her lunch.

"Thanks a lot!" Martha Ann hissed at her. "Now, look what you've done." She stabbed the cooked carrots on her plate and stuffed them into her mouth. Connie looked at her and shrugged, which made her even madder. The mouthful of carrots didn't go down very easily. She put down her fork and, rising quickly and picking up her tray, she muttered, "See you later."

At the supper table Mrs. Pierce asked the usual questions about their day. Martha Ann had little to say, but, fortunately, Brad was full of news about plans for the upcoming school carnival, so Martha Ann hoped no one would notice. She could never let her father know what had happened at lunchtime.

That night as Martha Ann got ready for bed, there was a tap on her door, and her mother came in.

"Something's wrong, sugar. I can tell. Do you want to talk about it?"

Martha Ann plopped down on the edge of her bed and put

her face in her hands. "Oh, Mom, it was awful. Connie mentioned about those girls that got killed yesterday when we were having lunch, and Sandra said she was a nigger-lover, and they all got up and left the table." Sobs made it difficult to get the words out. "Sandra said I was probably one too. Mom, what am I going to do? No one's going to speak to me anymore, all 'cause of Connie."

Mrs. Pierce patted her daughter, clucked, and said, "There, there," while Martha Ann's tears poured out. After a while Martha Ann's shoulders stopped shaking with her weeping and her mother handed her a tissue.

"What should I do, Mom? What can I do?" Martha Ann asked, looking up at her mother.

"Now, listen to me, darlin'. This is the South, and the way we live is separate from the Negroes. Our lives will never be mixed with theirs. You have to look out for yourself. Connie made herself a big mistake talking about the Negroes. That won't ever do anything to help them. It'll only hurt a body with their own kind. So, Connie needs to go to Sandra and say she realizes she made a mistake, that she's sorry, and say that she won't be bringing that subject up again."

Martha Ann shook her head. "Connie'll never do that."

"Well, you can't be worrying about Connie then. You gotta let Sandra know that you and Connie have different opinions."

"But, Mom, Connie was right. She was saying that it's a bad thing about those girls, that's all. That it was wrong to bomb the church."

"'Course it was. But she didn't need to be going 'round talking 'bout it."

"Mom, you were upset about it when you told us. You stood up to Daddy."

Martha Ann's mother flushed. "And I shouldn't a' done that."

"But, Mom—"

"There's no 'buts' about it, Martha Ann, unless you're wanting to be an outcast the rest of your life, and never be invited to parties, or asked on a date, or even have a friend to talk to. You can't do a blessed thing about the coloreds, so don't jeopardize your whole life for a lost cause." Mrs. Pierce gave Martha Ann a final pat on her shoulder. She walked to the door, stopped, and turned back. "Believe me, sugar, I know about such things. In this world, you'll survive only if you put aside those feelings that are different from those folks who are running things. That's a hard lesson, but the sooner you learn it, the better."

Martha Ann stared at the door a long time after her mother had closed it behind her, a cold, hard sadness enveloping her whole body and spirit.

CHAPTER TWELVE

Peace, may it dwell in our hearts, our homes, and in our world.
Traditional Christmas card greeting

December 1964
LETITIA

It's almost Christmas again. I hope this one is better than last year's. Last year we were still reeling from the deaths of those girls at the Sixteenth Street Baptist Church. I dreamt about Mama Lucy again last night. Whenever I dream about her, she's always telling me not to be so angry. In my dreams she tells me to be strong and that anger only distracts a person from what they should be doing. I know that's what she would be saying if she were still here, but it's hard to follow that advice.

Sam's a lot like Mama Lucy. So many of his friends are mad about being nonviolent. They think we should fight back, but Sam explains how that only makes things worse. Even though I know that, I want to fight back too.

Since I'm the one Mama Lucy gave the locket to, I should be more like her. I try; I really do. I work hard in school to get the best grades so I can go to college and become a teacher. I'm determined about that. So is Mae, but she wants to go to the University of Alabama. She thinks that's the way she can be out in front of any civil rights struggle. I want the results, but I don't care to lead the way like that. I understand from a long-ago conversation with Mama Lucy, when she read to me from the Bible, that we all have different ways to serve the Movement, and that we'll know what we should do. I don't see being one of the few blacks that integrate the university is my way. Mae and I almost got into an argument about that last week. Mama let us bake brownies, and we had taken a plate of them up to my room. Sam was out, and Etta was playing downstairs.

Mae started it all by saying, "Only a year and a half and we'll graduate. Why won't you come to Alabama with me? We could be roommates."

"Mae, you know the university is a white school. I'm not going to any white school where everybody will look down on me."

"There are Negroes that go there already, and more will go all the time. How can it ever change from being a white school if Negroes don't start going there?"

"Well, that's true, but I'm not gonna be one of those Negroes. I'm going to Miles College here at home, and that's that." I reached for another brownie. I felt a flush rising in my face. How could Mae imply that I didn't work for civil rights? I wanted to remind her that I almost had to drag her to that first march.

"But, Letitia, it's our generation that has to make the difference."

That really made me mad. "I did make a difference. I got hosed, didn't I? I can still feel the sting of that water. And remember those dogs?"

Mae looked surprised at the angry tone of my voice. "Sure you did, and I did too. That's what we needed to do then. Integrating the state colleges is what we need to be doing now."

"And what good would that do anyway? Things will never change here in the South. Look at what happened after we all marched. The whites went back on what they said they would do, and we had to have more protests. And the more protests we have, the madder blacks and whites get, and the worse off we are." I was really riled up then.

"Whoa," Mae said, putting a hand on my arm. "Settle down, girl. Look at all we have accomplished."

"Like what?"

"Like the poll tax that kept so many Negroes from voting has been abolished. Like President Johnson passing the Civil Rights Act of 1964."

"But look at the riots at the Democratic Convention last summer. And what about those three civil rights workers who were killed in Mississippi?"

Mae sighed, "Yeah, those things happened."

"See? Things will never really change in the South."

Mae shook her head. "I can't believe that. They'll never change if we do nothing, if we let things go on the way they are. You convinced me of that once. But, Letitia, things have changed. There are no more colored-only water fountains and everything. It's gonna take time."

Then it was my turn to sigh. Somehow we'd changed sides. My anger had pushed my desire to be part of any demonstrations out of the way. "I know. But here's what makes me mad. We can get laws changed and start doing things with Negroes and whites together, yet attitudes won't change. The white will always hate the Negro, and the Negro will never trust the white."

"When did you become such a cynic?"

That comment brought me up short. When did I? I used to be such an optimist. I shook my head sadly. "I guess it's happened since the Movement. Before that, I didn't realize how badly the whites treated us. The Movement really opened my eyes."

"The problem is that you don't know any white people, and you think all whites are the same. Think about how many whites have joined the demonstrations. You saw all those white people who came to the girls' funerals, who tried to let us know how sorry they were. Letitia, you're showing the same attitude as those whites who are against us because we're Negroes. You think all whites are mean, and they're not."

Her words hit me like a slap. In my heart I knew she was probably right, but I didn't care. I wasn't ready to admit it. I sat rigid and silent, my arms wrapped around myself.

"Letitia." Her voice was softer. "If you come to the university with me, you'll get to know some white people. You'll see that they're people like us, some good, some bad."

For some reason, I felt tears burn in my eyes, but I held them back. There was a kind of lump in my throat so I didn't answer Mae. I had the feeling that this is the kind of thing Mama Lucy might have said to me, so I took her words into my heart and knew I'd think about them later.

I put my hand to my throat and feel the solid metal of the locket. I don't want to deal with the struggle of the civil rights movement. I want to think about Damon, and dances, and parties. I want Mae and me to think the same way, feel the same about everything, like we always have.

That night I dream about Mama Lucy. We're walking through Kelly Ingram Park. It's springtime, and Mama Lucy is pointing out the flowers that are coming up through the hard, brown earth.

"Looka' these flowers, sugar. They know it's spring and time to come show their faces to the sun."

I simply smile at her in response.

"It's all in the Good Book, you know. It say, 'To everything there's a season. A time to live and a time to die.' Umhmm. It's all there in the Bible."

I walk in silence beside her. Because of her I know that scripture.

"That's true in all a' life, baby girl. All a' life. Like now is the season for you to be growing up, to be getting that education. To be finding that man who's right for you."

I stay silent. I feel like she's trying to tell me something important.

"And for our whole country, things are changing. No more lynching, no more Klan. No sir, this is the time for doing right, for letting all the coloreds have equal chances."

"Are you saying I should work in the Movement again, Mama Lucy?"

"You got to decide that for your ownself. But I am saying that you need to look at everything that's happening and find your own place in it. Don't let your emotions get in the way. Use them to make you strong."

When I wake up, that's all I remember of the dream. Or was it a dream? Sometimes Mama Lucy is so real to me, I don't feel like she's passed.

Mae and I talk about the Movement lots of times. One day she begins by saying, "You know, Letitia, back when we marched with Rev. Bevel and all them, back a year ago May?"

"Yeah?"

"Well, do you remember I told you I'd never march again?"

"Uh huh," I say, wondering what she's getting at.

"I've done a lot of thinking all year, and I've changed my mind."

"You have?" I am surprised by her statement and her change of heart.

"Yeah. I think there's a way I can support the Movement. I really care about things like voter rights now. We have a lot more work to do."

I nod. "I agree. But, for me, I still feel the best thing to do is work hard to become a good teacher, to be the best teacher for Negro kids. If I become a foot soldier like you're talking about, and get arrested, that could hurt my chances for being a teacher. I can't afford to do that."

Mae smiles at me. "I understand." Those simple words remind me why she's my best friend. She lets me be me.

December 1964
MARTHA ANN

The bell rang for the end of school, and boys and girls erupted from all the doors along the hall. The level of excitement that seemed to reverberate off the walls testified to the fact that this was the last day of school before Christmas vacation.

Martha Ann made her way quickly to the gym. Already many were there, talking and laughing together. Martha Ann saw Molly, Sandra, and the others coming in, and hurried over to them.

"Are you coming to the dance with Tommy?" asked Sandra.

"No," Martha Ann answered. "He said he'd see me there, but we don't have a date. What about you?"

"Oh, Larry asked me weeks ago."

"Students," called Mrs. Roose above the din of the crowd. "Give me your attention." They crowded around her waiting for their assignments. Martha Ann and most of her friends were spending Friday afternoon and Saturday decorating the gym for the dance. It was one of the favorite events of the year. Martha Ann thought there was always something magical about coming into the gym when it was transformed by decorations and lighting, and the feeling that one was entering a winter fantasyland for the very first time. This new place had no connection to the echoes of balls bouncing and the smell of sweaty socks and sneakers. She loved the way something as plain as a high-school gym could become beautiful.

Saturday night Molly and Connie came over after an early supper carrying armfuls of crinolines and their dresses.

All three girls already had their hair rolled up on empty frozen orange juice cans. "I brought nail polish," announced Molly.

"Great." The three girls layered the shiny, red polish on each others' nails while discussing the boys they knew would be there.

"Do you think Tommy will ask you to go steady tonight?" asked Molly.

Martha Ann paused. She had dreamt of that happening, but she still wasn't sure of Tommy. "Maybe. Maybe not," she finally answered.

The time flew by as the girls prepared for the big dance.

Martha Ann finished her final touch to her hair. Her room had become a jumble of girls' clothes, hair rollers, and all the paraphernalia that went with getting ready for a big evening. Smiling at each other, they headed downstairs. The skirt of Martha Ann's red chiffon dress floated over three crinolines as she descended. Mr. Pierce stood in the hallway waiting to drive them to the dance.

"Why, look at you beautiful girls." He smiled at them and tossed the car keys in the air. "Your limousine is waiting."

Martha Ann laughed and grabbed up her jacket.

Her mother came out from the kitchen, her apron still tied around her waist. Her expression became wistful as she clasped her hands in front of her. "Well, look at the three of you. Y'all will be the prettiest girls there."

The girls flushed with pleasure. Earlier they had creamed their faces. They had washed, conditioned, and rolled their hair and sat under the bulging hood of the hair dryer. They had helped each other with their makeup—a light touch of blush, a dusting of powder, some mascara, and lipstick. And now, with their special dresses, they did feel pretty. The evening lay before them like an unexplored road, full of the promise of adventure.

"Let's go," said Mr. Pierce.

"You need a chauffeur's cap to wear, Harold," remarked Martha Ann's mother.

"Mom, please. It's bad enough we have to have our parents drive us."

As if that reminded Mrs. Pierce, she said, "And your dad will bring y'all home right afterwards, right, Molly?"

"Yes, ma'am."

The three girls bundled into the backseat of the car, squishing fluffy crinolines around them. With Mr. Pierce in the front seat, the girls didn't say much. Their secret expectations for the evening had all been shared in the privacy of Martha Ann's room.

Mr. Pierce pulled the car in the drive for the high-school gym. The car lights highlighted a group of four Negro boys and their dates approaching the gym doors.

"My God! Are they letting those niggers go to your dance?" He slammed his foot on the brake, and the car jolted to a stop.

"Daddy!" squealed Martha Ann.

"It was bad enough letting you go to the same school as the colored, but I am not letting any daughter of mine dance with them."

Martha Ann's face was bright red. She was so mortified she could hardly sputter out the words. "Daddy, they brought those guys in for the football team. They stay to themselves. I promise you they won't be dancing with any white girls. We don't even talk to them."

"You're not going in there with them, and that's final."

Martha Ann looked at her friends with desperation. "Daddy, you can't mean that. We've looked forward to this dance. You can't forbid me to go. You can't!"

"I can't say anything about what your friends do, but I sure as hell can say about you, and I'm taking you home."

"Daddy, no!" Martha Ann wailed.

Molly opened the car door and started out. "Thank you for the ride, Mr. Pierce," she said politely over her shoulder as she stepped to the curb.

Connie gave Martha Ann a quick, sad glance, then stepped out also. "Yes, thank you for the ride."

Out of the corner of her eye, Martha Ann spied Tommy leaning against the wall, waiting for her arrival. *No! No, this can't be happening!*

Martha Ann slid toward the open car door. Her father's hand reached out and grabbed her arm. "You're not going anywhere, girl. Close that door."

"No! I'm going to the dance." Her breath came out in gasps as she tried to twist out of the viselike hold her father had on her arm.

Keeping his hand around her arm, her father slid across the seat until he could reach the door with his free hand. He slammed the door shut, and Martha Ann fell across the seat sobbing.

"You've ruined my life!" she screamed at him. "I hate you! I'll never be able to face anyone at school again."

Mr. Pierce gripped the steering wheel, and the car shot forward. "I don't care. It's my job to keep you safe from niggers, and I mean to do that."

Martha Ann shook with rage. She felt a terrible pain in her chest. She didn't think she could ever go back to Shades Valley High.

CHAPTER THIRTEEN

Anger is a wind which blows out the lamp of the mind.
Roger Green Ingersoll, *Quotations Book*

Spring 1965
LETITIA

Every day this week as we walk home from school, Mae's been urging me to go with her to the next demonstration. It's going to be a march from Selma to our capital. I think the idea is to confront Gov. Wallace. Like that'll do any good. I don't know why Mae keeps bugging me about going. She should know by now that I'm through with being in demonstrations for civil rights.

"Letitia, listen to me," she goes on one afternoon. "Each little part we do and win helps the whole civil rights movement. Someday, things are going to be really equal and fair for us. That'll make all the hard times worth it."

I glance at her with a scowl on my face. "I don't see any changes. What's happened since old Bull Connor turned those hoses on us, huh? My daddy's still worried that if he doesn't grovel to the white boss, he'll get fired. My mama still hauls herself over the mountain twice a week to do that uppity Miz Pierce's dirty work."

Mae laughs. "You don't really know her. How do you know she's uppity?"

"I know all right. She thinks she's being so good by sending her daughter's old rags home with Mama 'cause she thinks we so poor we can't buy our own clothes."

"Letitia, you always resent that now, and I don't get it. Those are nice things she gives you. Can't you simply appreciate them? I remember how much you liked some things she sent when we were younger."

"'Cause then I didn't know any better. I don't want any prissy white girl's clothes."

Mae shakes her head. "Well, let's get back to the Movement. Things are changing, you know."

"Yeah, a lot has happened since we got hosed back in May of 1963. The biggest thing is that President Kennedy got shot. We believed he finally could see all the injustices going on in the South, and we thought he would do something about them. And what happens? Some white man kills him."

We're both quiet for a few moments after that, remembering. It was a terrible time. For the next few days afterwards, we had the TV going whenever we were home, just watching all about the funeral and everything. So sad.

Mae breaks our silence. "But you gotta admit, one good thing that happened, though, is that President Johnson passed the Civil Rights Act. It says there can't be any more discrimination because of race. That's a law now, Letitia. It gives us something to stand on when we're fighting for our rights."

"Sure, and I heard President Johnson say that should end all these racial problems here in the South. But you know what? I haven't seen many changes at all down here. Oh, sure, we Negroes can go into restaurants and lots of other places now, but the whites here don't seem to treat us any differently."

"That'll happen someday. At least we have a start. We've started integrating the schools."

"But that's kinda scary. I'm glad I can stay at Parker. I haven't really talked to anyone who's had to go to a white school, but I can imagine what it's like."

"Well, the world is becoming a better place, whether or not you can see it, Letitia. After all, Dr. King got the Nobel Peace Prize. That's a big thing. He was the youngest person ever to receive the award. He wouldn't have gotten that if the work of the Movement wasn't important."

"He's not young; he's thirty-five years old!"

Mae laughs again. "Honestly, you have become the most negative person I know. Can't you see good in anything?"

I scowl even more. I didn't used to be this way. I really don't want Mae and me to grow apart, but I can't seem to help myself. I put my hand to my locket. I know what Mama Lucy would say: "Get over yourself, girl."

"The Selma march for voters' rights is gonna be this Sunday. You won't miss any school or anything. Won't you come with me? They'll be shuttling us from the church."

"Mae, I'm not going. Stop asking me."

Mae shrugs. "OK, suit yourself. You'll miss being part of history, but if that's the way you want it."

I finally smile and pat her on the shoulder. "I'm glad you finally get it." One of the nicest things about close friends, I think, is that you really can disagree without it hurting your friendship. I hope Mae keeps feeling that way.

I'm uneasy all Sunday from the moment I first wake up. After church and our Sunday dinner, I walk down to Kelly Ingram Park. The leaves on the trees are budding out, that soft, gentle green. There's a little breeze, and I can hear it softly stirring the leaves. I brought a book, *The Shoes of the Fisherman*, and I sit under one of the trees, resting my back against the trunk. I can't concentrate, though. I'm worried about Mae.

I probably shouldn't have come to the park today of all days because it sure doesn't do anything to help to have the memories of violence slipping out. This has always been our park, but I don't love it here like I used to. It's spoiled. Those police and firemen might as well have peed on every bush and tree, marking their territory like a big, old dog. The longer I sit here, the madder I get. I finally give up and walk back home.

Daddy talked to me about my anger once. He said that he

and Mama were worried about how angry I stayed because of Bull Connor and the way he treated Negroes. Mama may have been worried about me, but she carries the same kind of anger inside her. I've seen it. Daddy is more like Mama Lucy and Sam. They're strong inside, but not because of anger. I wish I could be more like that.

When the news comes on that evening, we watch, Mama, Daddy, and me. Etta is here, of course, but she doesn't pay any attention to the news. Sam is gone. He graduated last year and joined the Marines.

Then, there it is, the Edmund Pettus Bridge out of Selma and all the marchers. I recognize Hosea Williams of SCLC and John Lewis of SNCC leading the marchers. They amble along, many dressed in suits, not seeming to mind the overcast weather. Suddenly, the police wade into the crowd, swarming over them. They start beating everyone with nightsticks, and they throw tear gas in. Some police on horseback ride into the crowd, not caring who gets trampled. I gasp at the terrible scenes. We can hear the screams and cries, see people staggering around, bleeding and dazed. I frantically search for Mae but don't see her. The newscaster says that the sheriff had ordered all white men over twenty-one to come in that morning to be deputized, then he calls it "Bloody Sunday." No one gets up to turn off the TV at the end of the news. We sit in silent horror, not even having words for each other.

Finally, I turn to my father. "And you wonder why I'm so angry"—my voice trembling as much as I am.

Daddy only shakes his head.

Later, when I know the shuttles are due back at the church, I go down to meet them. I have to know how Mae is. I pace back and forth as the first of several cars arrive. The evening is cool. The sky turns from pink to gray as dusk settles around us. Those of us waiting talk quietly, if at all. Mae doesn't get out of any of the first cars. As the marchers arrive and are greeted by loved ones, we hear snatches of the story, see bandaged wounds, bruised limbs, torn clothing. With each testimony to the violence, I feel my heart breaking a little more.

The last station wagon arrives, and Mae slips out of the back seat. After her family has held her close, I step up and hug her. We don't say a word. What is there to say that we don't already know in our hearts? Mae's arm has a huge bruise, but that seems to be her only injury. I'm relieved about that. Slowly, we all make our way home, hearts heavy, some more determined than ever to keep marching, some doubting that things will ever change.

I'm surprised—but I guess I shouldn't be—that there is another march from Selma on Tuesday. Dr. King leads this, and they only go across the bridge, have a prayer service, and go back. Then, they plan a huge march for March 21. Mae is gonna march again, and before she goes, she keeps trying to get me to go too.

"Rev. Bevel's gonna be there," she tells me.

"If anyone can get me to march again, it would be Rev. Bevel, but, even so, I'm not going, and I think y'all are crazy to be part of it."

"But, Lettie, this is all about voting rights. Whites don't want us to vote, because the vote holds power, but we've got to be able to register and vote."

"I know all that, Mae. You know I do."

"Don't you remember Rev. Bevel telling us how most places in Alabama have limited times when Negroes can go to get registered, and then they have to pass tests that are pretty much impossible to pass?"

I roll my eyes at her in exasperation. "Yes, I remember. I know it, but I am not gonna be part of a demonstration like that ever again."

Mae ignores me. "Listen to me, girl. I read in the paper that in Dallas County, where Selma is, fifty-seven percent of the population is Negro, fifteen thousand people, but only a hundred and thirty Negroes are registered to vote. When I see things like that, how can we not demonstrate?"

I shake my head. "I can understand why you're so committed to protest, but I just can't do it." I pause. "Maybe I will next time." We're almost to our houses.

Mae smiles at me and goes her way.

This time, when they march, there are thousands of soldiers and National Guard along the way to protect the marchers, and they get all the way from Selma to the capital in Montgomery. I'm glad, and I'll admit to a little twinge of conscience about not going.

Late December - Spring 1965
MARTHA ANN

Martha Ann was beginning to think that perhaps things had smoothed out between her parents. The problem was as soon as she'd think that, there would be another violent outburst. Her father truly frightened her when he was angry, and when he acted OK, she didn't trust him. How could he have forgotten the cursing, yelling, and throwing things that happened out of the blue? Of course, she didn't think she would ever forgive him for mortifying her in front of her friends at the Christmas Dance.

Her mother came into her room one evening and, sitting next to Martha Ann on the bed, took her hand and said, "Sugar, we need to talk."

"What's the matter?" asked Martha Ann.

"You know very well," her mother answered, a sad smile on her face. "You and your father live in the same house. You can't go on like this forever."

"Mom! He ruined my life, made me the laughingstock of my class. I'll never be able to face people at school again."

"You think that now, but it won't be that way. Use this holiday time to do things with your friends. When you start back to school, it will all be forgotten. You'll see."

"My friends will never do things with me again."

"Of course they will, or they're not really friends. You've talked to Connie and Molly on the phone. Why not ask them to go to the movies sometime?"

"Well, they did say something about going to see A Hard Day's Night again."

Mrs. Pierce smiled. "Make some plans to go."

Martha Ann paused. She really did want to see that Beatles movie again. "Oh, OK," she finally said.

"Martha Ann, you need to forgive your father too."

"Why? Why do you forgive him for the way he treats you? He's a bully, Mom." Martha Ann's eyes filled with tears. "Why do you stay with him?"

Mrs. Pierce's lips trembled, and she stayed quiet for a moment. "You'll understand when you're older."

"I'll never understand. Aren't you afraid he might hurt you sometime?" Martha Ann had never dared talk to her mother this way before, but it was hard to ignore the broken plates, glasses, and lamps he had thrown in anger.

Her mother stood up and clasped her hands in front of her. "Sometimes, a person has no choices. I have to make things work. I want you to have choices, Martha Ann. That's why it's so important for you to get your education. You won't be at home many more years, but as long as you're here, please try to make it work. For all our sakes, please get along with your father." She dropped her hands and waited a moment, her gaze steady on her daughter.

Martha Ann sighed. "All right. I'll try."

With a brisk nod, Mrs. Pierce turned and walked out of the room.

Martha Ann sat quietly for a while. *But I won't like it.*

Beatlemania. The virus had affected all of the United States, and Birmingham, Alabama, was no exception. Martha Ann and her friends had been infected ever since their first glimpse of the shaggy-haired British foursome on television the year before.

TURNER

They had seen the movie *A Hard Day's Night* three times. Now, they were gathered in Molly's bedroom playing 45s, especially "I Want to Hold Your Hand." The three friends collapsed on Molly's bed after trying some of the latest dance steps.

"I hope they have some good records at the dance next weekend."

"They will, don't worry," Molly said, getting up and going to her bureau. Rummaging in her top drawer she pulled out a pack of Newports and returned to the bed. She held out the cigarettes to Martha Ann and Connie.

"Won't your mom and dad be mad?" asked Martha Ann.

"No, they won't know. They never come in my room."

Connie shook her head. "My mom said that there's a new report out that smoking causes cancer."

Molly tossed her head in dismissal. "They're always saying something we like causes cancer. You can't pay any attention to that." She tossed the pack onto the bed, lit her cigarette, inhaled, and slowly blew out the smoke.

Martha Ann and Connie looked at each other, shrugged, and took a cigarette.

"Is your daddy gonna let you go to the dance?" Molly asked.

Martha Ann's face flushed. "Of course," she answered brusquely. "The only reason he didn't let me go to that Christmas Dance last year was because he saw those Negro boys go in. He was only trying to protect me." That's what her mother had said one time anyway.

"That was awful. We knew just how you felt."

Martha Ann nodded. Her heart raced a little faster as she remembered that night. She hated her father then, but what could she do? Since that night, she lived for the time when she'd be free of his control. Still, she didn't want her friends judging her father too harshly. It was embarrassing.

"I was so mad at my daddy that night that I seriously thought about running away from home."

"Why didn't you?" asked Molly.

Martha Ann paused. The truth was that she had thought about climbing out her window and into the tree that grew close to the house. It would have been an easy climb down the rest of the way to the ground. But leaning on her windowsill, she pictured in her mind's eye looking back at her house. She imagined the soft, yellow light coming through the windows, drawing her back to its warmth, and she decided that she couldn't—didn't really want to—leave.

She almost smiled as she confessed, "I couldn't think of any place to run to."

The girls laughed. "Well, it's a good thing you're going with Tommy this time," said Connie.

"I was afraid Tommy would never have anything to do with me after that," Martha Ann said.

"When we told him what had happened, he said he was glad somebody would take a stand against the Negroes." Connie gave Martha Ann a look that said exactly what she thought about Tommy for his views. Martha Ann squirmed a little under her friend's gaze.

"It still seems odd to see the coloreds at school. I only have a class with one, and he sits way in the back and doesn't say anything." Molly got up to put on another record. "Should I play 'House of the Rising Sun'?"

Martha Ann stretched out, grinding out her cigarette on the empty cookie plate beside the bed. "No, play 'Let It Be Me.'" She closed her eyes and imagined dancing with Tommy's arms around her.

A light tap on the door, and they scurried to hide the cigarettes. Molly's mother came in, and the serious way she looked at Martha Ann made Martha Ann sit up straight, expecting something bad.

"Martha Ann, honey, your daddy just called. Your brother's been in an accident and they're all on the way to the hospital. You're to stay here with us until they know what's going to happen."

"Brad? What happened?" Martha Ann's stomach dropped and landed in a knot. No one in her family had ever been in the hospital. How bad was this?

Molly's mother looked away a moment. "He was riding his bike, your mom said. Riding home. Someone didn't see him and hit him."

"With their car? He was hit by a car?" Martha Ann felt a shock through her whole body. She pictured Brad, lying in a heap in the middle of the road, bleeding and unconscious. "I want to go to the hospital too. I need to be there!" Tears poured down her face.

Mrs. Kelly sat by Martha Ann on the bed, putting her arms around her. "There, now. I know how upset you must be, but your dad said it would be best for you to wait here until they know something. I'm sure they'll call you as soon as possible."

"But . . . but I want to be with my family," she stammered.

"I know you do, honey. And as soon as they call, we'll take you to them. For right now, though, it's good for you to be here with your friends."

"Yeah," said Connie, sitting on the other side of Martha Ann and gently patting her arm. "We're here and we'll help you. Don't worry."

Mrs. Kelly gave Martha Ann a squeeze and stood up. "That's right. How about if I bring up some cookies? Do y'all want a Coke Cola or anything?" She looked around at the girls. "Molly, come help me get some Coke Colas."

The next few hours passed in slow agony for Martha Ann. Not knowing what was happening to her brother terrified her. She pictured every kind of horrible scenario imaginable. Molly and Connie tried to distract her with conversation and music, but nothing really helped.

Finally, the girls heard the phone ring and rushed to the top of the stairs. Mrs. Kelly came from the kitchen after a few minutes. "Martha Ann, we'll take you to the hospital now. Your brother is still in surgery, but your mom wants you to be there waiting with them."

Martha Ann rushed down the stairs, calling good-bye to her friends over her shoulder.

Mrs. Kelly went in the hospital with her, although she had trouble keeping up. In the waiting room, Martha Ann rushed to her mom and dad, and they stood quickly and folded her close to them.

"How is he?" Martha Ann sobbed. "What happened?"

"Someone turning the corner just didn't see him. Brad was riding his bike home. I don't know what happened. He didn't see the car or something—I don't know." Her mother sat on the green couch, pulling Martha Ann next to her, tears ending her words. Her dad held on to Martha Ann's other hand and sat down too.

"His leg was broken. They're fixing that in surgery now," he told her.

Martha Ann looked at her father. She'd never seen him so pale, look so worried. "But that doesn't sound too bad. That's not too bad, is it?" she asked, a note of desperation in her voice.

Her father squeezed her hand tighter. "No, that part's not so dangerous." He paused. "What we're most concerned about is the head injury. They can't tell yet how serious that is."

"Head injury? Oh, Daddy, no!"

"Now, sugar, he's in good hands. We have lots of confidence in the doctors. We've called the church, and he's already on the prayer chain. Everything that can be done is being done."

Martha Ann leaned against her father's chest, and he put his arms around her as she wept.

"We'll be OK, honey, we'll be OK," he kept saying as he held her close.

And, somehow, in his secure embrace she began to feel some peace.

CHAPTER FOURTEEN

Sing a song full of the faith that the dark past has taught us. Sing a song full of the hope that the present has brought us.
James Weldon Johnson, *"Lift Every Voice and Sing"*

May 1966
LETITIA

My senior year is almost over. I can hardly believe it. I'm happy, excited, and scared, all at the same time. When I get home from school today, the letter I've been waiting for is there. Of course, I call Mae right away, after Mama and I finish jumping up and down and hugging.

"Mae, I made it! I got into Miles College. I'm so excited."

I can hear Mae's familiar chuckle bubbling over the phone line. "Well, that's no surprise. You're only one of the top students at Parker."

"What a relief. I thought this acceptance letter would never come."

"That's great, Lettie. I'm happy for you."

Mae and I had already gotten our acceptances from the University of Alabama, and even though she knows I want to go to Miles, she keeps pestering me to change my mind and be her roommate at Alabama. I don't want to go to such a big school, especially because it's pretty much a white school.

"With my scholarship and living at home, I can really do this. This is a dream come true."

Mae laughs out loud. "I know it, girl. There'll be no stopping you now."

I have to laugh too, I feel so good. Then I think about our not being together. "Yeah, but I'm gonna miss you, Mae. How am I gonna get along without you?"

There's silence on the phone for a minute. All the laughter has gone out of Mae's voice when she answers, "Oh, I expect you'll manage, and I guess I will too, but it'll be hard. We'll have to find time to write each other, and I'll come home lots of weekends."

"But it won't be the same, will it?"

"Maybe not. Still, I'm excited about your news."

After we hang up, I'm still thinking about starting a new life as a college student. I go into the kitchen where Mama is sitting at the table shelling peas for supper. She looks up as I plop into a chair opposite her.

"Now why are you wearing that down-in-the-mouth expression when you just been accepted to the college? You the first one in all the family to go to a college. You should be shouting out loud." She looks down at the pod in her hand and deftly scoops the peas into the bowl.

"I am happy, Mama, but I'm sad thinking about not seeing Mae every day."

Her hands pause as she pulls the next pod up, and she looks up at me again. "'Course you are, sugar. Moving on is one of the hardest lessons of life, but, you know, it's not nearly as hard as standing still and going nowhere would be." She busies herself with the peas again.

I absentmindedly pick up some pods and begin to help. "Yeah, I know."

We sit in a comfortable silence for a while until all the peas are done. Mama gets up and carries the bowl to the sink. As she swishes the water over them, she says, "I'm worried a mite about your daddy. I'm afraid he's got the sugar disease like Mama Lucy. He's gonna see the doctor today about it."

My heart skips a beat as my head shoots up. "Mama, why didn't you tell me?"

Without turning around, she says, "I'm telling you now."

"But how sick is he? Is he gonna be all right?"

"He'll be OK; don't you be getting in a stew about it. If he do have it, they'll give him the medicine to use. It'll be OK. I just wanted to let you know, prepare your mind for it, that's all."

"Oh, Mama, I can't stand to think of Daddy being sick, 'specially not with diabetes like Mama Lucy."

She turns to face me. "Then don't think about it, sugar. Think about getting accepted at that great college, think about going to the prom next Saturday with Damon, think about Sam getting home from that Vietnam place in a few days. 'Member what Mama Lucy always used to say? 'Use your mind to take you where you want to go.' You can do that, can't you?"

I get up and cross the small distance to my mama. I hug her tight. Even though she didn't finish high school, I think she's a pretty smart person.

Up in the bedroom Etta and I share, I pull out my diary from the drawer. I have a lot to write about. I start out by writing *Everything changes, and that's a good thing and a bad thing.*

Sam gets home, his two years in the Marine Corps over. He looks different to me, grown up, tall and slim. He seems different too, like he carries a sadness inside or something—maybe it's anger. I thought he would be like his old self at dinner, talking a mile a minute, telling us all about his adventures. But it isn't like that at all.

"I fixed all your favorite foods, honey," Mama says. "How come you not eating?"

"I'm not very hungry, Mama," he says. He pushes his black-eyed peas around with his fork.

"Tell us about what you done over in Vietnam, son. What was it like?" Daddy asks.

"There's really nothing to say."

Etta and I exchange looks. This isn't like our brother at all.

"Did you like the other guys in your unit?" I ask.

"Sure. They was good guys." He picks up the chicken leg and takes a bite.

"Did you go on patrols like we seen on the TV?" says Daddy.

"Um hmm." Sam nods his head.

Mama pushes the bowl of greens closer to Sam. "Here, son, have some more." Her expression carries that worried look she gets sometimes.

"No thanks."

Daddy keeps on, "Did you do Search and Destroy like we heard about?"

Sam puts down his fork and slowly looks around the table at all of us. "Why can't y'all understand? I don't want to talk about it. I'm not gonna talk about it." He slides back his chair and stands up. "I'm going out to see some friends. I'll see y'all later."

I don't know which is sadder, watching him leave or seeing how he limps now. None of us knew he'd been wounded. He'd only say that there was some shrapnel hit his leg, that it was nothing. It doesn't seem like nothing to me. After he leaves, we can't look at each other or I think we'd start crying. Sam isn't the same person he was before he went to Vietnam, and none of us know what to do about that.

I hear him come in late that night. He's stumbling around, and I wonder if he's drunk. Daddy gets up and comes out. I can hear them talking but I can't hear the words clearly. Some of Daddy's words are "no son of mine" and "in my house." Daddy's voice is getting louder and angrier. Hearing it puts a knot in my stomach. When Sam finally gets loud enough for me to understand his words, he's yelling "come back and treated like crap." I bunch the pillow over my head and try to sleep.

May 1966
MARTHA ANN

Martha Ann leaned back against the porch steps savoring the southern springtime. Connie plopped down two steps below her and stretched out her legs. "Boy, our senior year has really flown by," she said.

Martha Ann shook her head. "For me, it seemed like forever. What a year!"

"Yeah, I guess, with your brother and all."

"That was the biggest thing, of course, but so much more changed this past year."

"Like what?" Connie asked, picking a handful of grapes from the bowl between them.

"Oh, so many things. Like us, for instance."

"Us?"

"I mean our friendship. You've always been my friend, ever since first grade, but it wasn't till those weeks after Brad got hurt that I realized what a real friend you are. You always were there to listen when I was scared and to let me cry when I needed to."

Connie shifted uncomfortably in her seat. "That wasn't anything."

"But it was. It really was. Because of that, I felt like I could share everything with you." Martha Ann lowered her voice to add, "Even about what was happening with my dad."

The two girls sat in silence a moment. Martha Ann popped a grape in her mouth. "That helped me not feel like I was all alone, you know?"

Connie nodded. "Well, you made me feel like I wasn't all alone standing up to Sandra after that."

The screech of bike tires on the driveway made both girls look around.

"Brad, you know you shouldn't be riding so fast!" yelled Martha Ann.

Brad laughed as he dropped his bike to the ground.

"And don't leave your bike there where it could get run over," Martha Ann added.

"You're not the boss of me," he said as he went back and moved it to the grass.

Connie smiled. "Well, he seems completely recovered, doesn't he?"

"Mmhmm. Those first few days till we knew his head injury would heal seemed like weeks. Then all that time in the hospital and rehab. It's sure made a difference in our family."

"What do you mean?"

"Well," said Martha Ann, looking around and lowering her voice. "You know my mom. It was pretty hard for her. She had to get our help to come in three days a week. Really, it was Daddy who held us all together. He was always calm and strong, you know? He worked so hard at helping Brad get through all that, the rehab and everything." She shrugged. "Before all this, I only saw him as a dictator, a racist dictator. But, this year . . . this year, he was the one we all leaned on. He was so gentle and loving, but strong." Martha Ann flushed. Connie had seen her dad at his worst. Now, maybe, she'd see him in a better light. Shaking her head as if it was hard to believe, she added, "Ever since Brad's accident, Daddy has never had one of those violent outbursts. I don't understand what happened." Someday maybe she could talk to her mom about it. "Anyway, it was a hard year, but it's getting better."

"And soon we'll be off to college. I can't wait!" said Connie. "Are you sure you don't want to come to Auburn with me?"

Martha Ann laughed. "You know this could affect our friendship forever, but I am all set for the University of Alabama."

Connie patted her friend's hand. "Too bad. You've made the wrong choice."

"Mom's going to take me shopping for my prom dress later," Martha Ann said to change the subject. "She seems as excited over all the senior activities as I am."

"My mom, too. Do you think they're wishing they were girls again?" Connie asked.

Martha Ann shrugged, "Who knows? Maybe they remember how much fun it was when they went through it and want to be sure we're enjoying it too. Parents are funny sometimes."

"Yeah," Connie agreed.

Later that week Mrs. Pierce parked the car, and she and Martha Ann walked the half block to Pizitz Department Store. The air was heavy with the scent of spring, carrying the suggestion of flowering things and new growth. A few white clouds scudded across the sky, gently, without sending shadows.

"After we find your prom dress, we'll go to the lunchroom and get ourselves a little treat," Mrs. Pierce said. She had dressed up for this special outing, a small green pillbox hat perched on her head, matching the green trim of her dress, white-gloved hands firmly gripping her tan leather purse.

Martha Ann smiled at her mother. She had looked forward to this shopping trip for days, not only for getting a special dress for her last high-school prom, but also for sharing this time with her mother.

As Martha Ann and her mother looked through gown after gown among the racks of satin and organdy, she simply enjoyed the moment. Pulling out a pale blue gown with dainty cap sleeves and a long full skirt, she exclaimed, "This one!" and hurried to the dressing room to try it on.

Martha Ann carefully laid the dress bag with the pale blue formal gown over the chair next to her, as she and her mother sat down at the table in the Pizitz lunchroom.

"I love my dress, Mom, don't you?"

Removing her gloves and folding them on her purse, Mrs. Pierce nodded.

They placed their order for the prized crème puffs, coffee, and a Coca-Cola. Mrs. Pierce patted her daughter's hand. "This's been fun, darlin'. I can hardly believe you're graduating high school and going off to college."

Martha Ann smiled. "I can hardly believe it myself, Mom. It's such an exciting time. Next year will be so great, being in college. I only wish Connie weren't going to Auburn. If she went to Alabama we could be roommates."

"Well, your friendship'll surely last, no matter where you go to school. I think it will be a good experience for you to meet new people, make new friends."

"Do you ever wish you'd gone to college, Mom? You've always insisted that I go."

Mrs. Pierce sighed and glanced off a moment before returning her gaze to Martha Ann. "I wish a lot of things, honey. When I was your age, college wasn't even a possibility. Granny and Grandpa struggled so hard to make ends meet, and there were six kids to be fed and clothed. Since I was the oldest, they needed me to start working too. Not many women went to college in my day, especially those whose dads worked in the mills or the mines."

"Daddy works in the mills."

"Yeah, but your Daddy's in management. I'm thankful he makes the kind of money he does so we can have a nice home and send you children to college."

"I'm thankful too, Mom."

"Your daddy's worked hard to take care of this family. Don't you forget that."

Conversation lulled as the waitress brought the crème puffs and drinks. Mrs. Pierce added two heaping teaspoons of sugar to her coffee and took a sip as Martha Ann took a bite of her pastry, savoring the rich creamy filling.

"I know Daddy works hard, Mom, and he's been great this year, but why was he so . . . so . . ."

"So angry?" her mother interjected.

"Yeah."

"Your father," Mrs. Pierce began. "Your father's a complex man. He's a good man at heart. He loves his family, works hard, goes to church. But . . ." She paused. "But he is the way he was raised. Life was hard, rough. Remember, he grew up in the country on the farm. His family didn't have much, and it was a hard time for our country too. You had to be tough to survive. You had to make sure no one was going to get ahead of you, do better than you, or you might lose." She looked at Martha Ann. "How can I make you understand? You live in a different kind of world than he grew up in. Your daddy has had to fight for everything he has. All that he's earned, none of it came easy. He was so determined to get an education, to get a decent job. Once he told me that at college the others made fun of him 'cause of his accent and country ways, his poor clothes. He's a strong man, but he lives with fear, an unnecessary fear, that he might lose what he's gained. And fear does things to people."

Martha Ann listened quietly, trying to understand. "Is that why he hates Negroes so much? He's afraid they'll take his job?"

"Well, no colored man could ever be a manager, but probably part of it is his need to keep them in their place. Another part is that he was brought up to think the colored are truly inferior. I mean, there's scientific information out there about that. So, it's only natural that he feels superior to the coloreds and thinks they're dirty and can't learn, things like that. Everyone around him did. It was as natural as breathing."

"But, Mom, when he used to get so angry at night, the yelling, that time you came into my room to stay safe—"

"I know. I know. It was hard to understand. He was going through a very bad time at work. There were cutbacks, layoffs. He was afraid he would lose his job, and we were all dependent on him."

"That's no excuse for taking it out on us with so much anger."

Mrs. Pierce sighed. "We're parents and we're supposed to do the right thing by our families, but we're human too, with all the faults humans have. When you're older, you'll understand."

Martha Ann shook her head as she forked another bit of crème puff. "Grown-ups always say that. I wish he hadn't been like that. How do we know it won't be like that again? I don't think I can ever really forgive him for not letting me go to the Christmas Dance last year."

"Honey, listen to me. Everything your daddy does, he does because he's looking out for you. That's what you need to be remembering. Lord, the most important thing we all need to do is forgive and forget. Believe me, it's the only way to get through life. Just forgive and forget."

Martha Ann looked at her mother for a moment and realized that for her mother, that was the only option. *I will never let myself get so trapped. Now I'm determined to get a college degree and have a career to fall back on!* "Well, Dad was pretty different this year with Brad," she said.

Tears came to her mother's eyes. "Yes," she said softly. "Yes, he was."

"I never thought about anything bad like when Brad got hurt happening to us."

"We never do. But things do happen, sugar. I pray you'll never have a difficulty in your life, but if you do, I hope you'll be like your daddy. Be strong."

Strong? Yeah, I'll be strong. But I'll do that by being able to stand up for myself, not like you by pretending everything is OK when it isn't.

Martha Ann sipped her drink. Memories of her dad flashed through her mind, his strong hands helping her learn to ride her bike, his driving her places she needed to go, his pitching softballs to her until her swing became strong and sure. Then she remembered the shouting, the way his eyes could look cold and angry, the night her mother ran into her room, the Christmas Dance. *Do I love him or hate him?* Now she was the one with no answer.

CHAPTER FIFTEEN

But I want you to know tonight that we as a people will get to the Promised Land. So, I'm happy tonight. I'm not worried about anything. I'm not fearing any man. Mine eyes have seen the glory of the coming of the Lord.

Dr. Martin Luther King, Jr., *speech, Memphis, Tennessee, April 3, 1968*

April 1968
LETITIA

Spring is such a beautiful season in Alabama without the moist heat that overpowers everything. We start with the redbud and tulip trees, the forsythia, then the azaleas and dogwoods, not to mention the daffodils, crocuses, and all those. The honeysuckle and jasmine send the most beautiful scent over the whole city. I should love spring in Alabama, but I don't. It reminds me too much of the Children's March and the Bloody Sunday march from Selma. Mae tells me to get over it. She always looks to a brighter future. Sam too.

"Letitia," he tells me, "we all could look at those things of the past and be mad as—" He stops. Since he got back from Vietnam, he's had to clean up his language around Mama. "As anything," he continues. "'Member how I was when I first got back from the Marine Corps?"

I nod. He wasn't the brother I knew at all.

"I was letting things I seen over there eat at me. Then to come back and find how little things had changed here. Those bad thoughts were taking over my whole self. The only relief was in drinking. What if I kept on like that, huh?"

"Yeah, we all worried about you. But, Sam, how do you stop thinking bad thoughts? How can I stop remembering how that hosing felt? How can I forget about all the bad things whites have done to us?"

Sam shakes his head. "I don't know what to tell you, Lettie. For me, it was a coupla' things. First, I thought about Mama Lucy, about her stories of how hard things were growing up for her. And I realized how far we'd really come, especially in the last few years. I didn't want her strength and courage to be for nothing, where I'd end up backsliding past everything."

I absentmindedly put my hand to my throat to clasp her locket, to feel its strength again.

"And something else made me change. Daddy. Daddy being sick with the sugar, thinking how hard he worked to get us all through high school, and now you in college. I decided I couldn't let him down. I had to get myself together and get a trade. I'm glad I'm learning plumbing now. I can make a good life from it."

Tears come to my eyes. It's been hard to see Daddy struggle with his health these days. He's been in the hospital three times, and each time I lived in fear that he wouldn't come back, just like Mama Lucy.

I know Sam's right about getting past these angry feelings, but, Lordy, I don't seem able to do it. Just when I make a little progress, bam! something else terrible happens.

Sam leans forward and starts again. "You know, Lettie, my dream when I was in high school was to join the Corps, then have them teach me a trade. But that sure as"—he almost slipped—"heck didn't happen. Those of us black guys come to think we were the dispensable ones 'cause they always put us in the front of the patrol, put us as point man. We weren't learning nothing but how to tramp through the jungle and get shot at. It was easy for us to feel mad. But one day, this black gunny sergeant took us aside.

"He told us, 'OK, you, mo . . .'—he almost slips again—'you

guys, why d'ya think the lieutenant makes you the point man, huh? Wise up. You think the man wants some dummy up there? No, that's the place for the smart guy, the man cool in a crisis. Most of you guys are street smart, not those white boys. You ain't there 'cause he devalues you. He puts you there 'cause he knows your worth.'"

"So what's your point?" I ask Sam.

"My point is that you can take what happens to you and look at it lots of different ways. You can choose to be mad about something or choose to put it in a positive light. You can choose, Lettie."

He sounds like Mama Lucy and Mae. Sometimes, I feel like they're all ganging up on me. I get up and wander outside.

That evening we all watch the news on the TV. Dr. King is on, making a speech. He says, "We've got some difficult days ahead. But it doesn't matter to me now because I've been to the mountaintop." I remember how he'd talk to us before the Children's March. I loved to hear him talk about going to the mountaintop and seeing the Promised Land. We all believed we'd get there, and the Promised Land meant freedom.

We'd been hearing how Dr. King was in Memphis to help. The Movement had made progress in that there was now legislation against the injustices. We had the Civil Rights Act of 1964 and the Voting Rights Act of 1965. But what hadn't changed were real opportunities for Negroes to get ahead, get good jobs, and get out of poverty. Daddy had explained to us what was happening.

"See, what's going on in Memphis is all over the South, maybe all over the whole country," Daddy began one evening after the news on TV mentioned about a garbagemen's strike. "Those men ain't got the same pay and benefits as the white ones, even though they doing the same job."

"How can they do that?" I asked, feeling that anger rising up again.

"They just do it, honey. I heard that when they got bad

weather and can't work, the whites still get paid, but not the Negroes."

Sam shook his head in disgust. "Then those two Negro garbagemen got crushed to death in the truck. The city government paid the families something, but not like they woulda done for whites, and they let the family know they didn't really have to do nothing 'cause they were Negro."

"That's right," said Daddy. "So, that's why they done ask Dr. King to come help them. 'Course, things ain't going so well yet, but he gonna get them turned 'round. You just watch."

Tonight, we're back in front of the TV. I'm taking a break from my homework. The Real McCoys is on when they break into the program and say that someone shot Dr. King while he was standing on the balcony of the Lorraine Motel in Memphis.

None of us can say a word, except Etta. She sees us all crying and keeps saying, "What's a matter? What happened?" We can't speak, and Mama sits next to her and hugs her tight.

I feel like someone hit me real hard in the chest and knocked all the air outta me. How can this be happening? *Not Dr. King. We can't lose Dr. King, or we've lost everything.*

They say they rushed him to the hospital, and we all are praying, I know, praying that they can fix him, that he won't die. I see Mama's mouth moving silently. I can almost feel the world holding its breath, praying for Dr. King.

But pretty soon, they come back on the TV and say he's been declared dead. Dead! How can God have let this happen? I put my hand 'round my locket, but it feels as cold as I am. Mama weeps like Sam, Etta, and me, but Daddy only shakes his head. "No more hope," he mumbles. "No more hope."

We spend the next few days watching the TV coverage all about it. We can hardly talk about it, just cry. President Johnson, he proclaims a National Day of Mourning, but I wonder if the whites are mourning Dr. King like we are. Our people are so mad that there's a lot of rioting 'round the country. I don't see what good that'll do, but I understand how that anger feels; I surely do.

The day of the funeral is April 9. Mama doesn't make us go to school. I don't think they're even having classes at Miles. We sit in front of the TV watching all the funeral, feeling like we're part of it.

It starts with a service at the Ebenezer Baptist Church in Atlanta. That's where Dr. King and his daddy were preachers. Then all the mourners walk down Central Avenue to Morehouse College, where Dr. King went to school. His coffin is in a plain ole farm wagon with two mules pulling the wagon. Thousands and thousands of people line the street and weep as he passes by. Sometimes they start singing the protest songs; they're like hymns to us now. One of the things they do at Morehouse is join hands and sing "We Shall Overcome." That's when I really feel my heart breaking because now I wonder if we ever will.

June 1968
MARTHA ANN

Martha Ann, Molly, and Connie felt their spirits soaring as they headed for the beach once school was out for summer vacation.

"How'd you ever get your folks to let you borrow the car?" Connie asked.

Molly laughed. "Sometimes, I feel like I can wrap my daddy 'round my little finger. He thinks y'all are so responsible that he caved in pretty easily."

"Well, this was a great idea," said Martha Ann. "My parents would never let me go for Spring Break. They hear too many stories of wild behavior. But, somehow, they think going this time of year is OK."

"So after two years, Connie, are you still liking Auburn?" Martha Ann asked. "Are you ready to transfer to Alabama and be my roomie?"

"No way. I love it there. Are you ready to come to Auburn?"

Martha Ann laughed, then grew serious. "Alabama is so big, though. Being there has made me realize what a sheltered life we all led here."

"You mean 'cause there's coloreds there?" asked Molly.

Martha Ann shook her head. "No, that's not it. I almost never see the blacks. There really aren't too many of them. There's so many students, all with different backgrounds. I don't know, it's a little overwhelming at first; I guess that's all I mean."

Molly sighed. "You know, I used to think that when we graduated from high school I'd finally be grown up. But I don't feel any different, do y'all? Maybe when I finish secretarial school and get a job and my own apartment, I'll feel like an adult. Now, I only feel the same as I did in high school, except I don't have y'all around."

"I think being away from home does help," Martha Ann answered. "Even though I may be doing the same kinds of things, my parents aren't watching over me, breathing down my neck about everything."

Connie nodded. "Well, you know my parents. They want us to think for ourselves, so since graduation they've pretty much let me make my own decisions. To tell you the truth, that's scary. A lot of responsibility. You have to think about the consequences of everything. It was a lot easier being a kid."

Molly's smile had a twinge of sadness to it. "I'm ready for that, but I don't think my parents are."

Martha Ann patted her hand. "Growing up sure isn't easy. I guess that's true for us and for our parents."

"But aren't you a little bit frightened by being away from home?" asked Molly. "When I heard about that guy, Richard Speck, killing all those nurses in their dorm, then that guy that shot a bunch of people from the tower at the University of Texas, Lord, I worried about y'all."

Connie brushed the thought away with a wave of her hand. "Those were isolated incidents. We're plenty safe. And think about it—we can wear miniskirts anytime we want without our parents fussing at us."

The three girls laughed, knowing the truth in her statement.

Martha Ann sighed as she changed the subject. "What worries me is all these demonstrations about the war in Vietnam. When they talk about the war, I don't see why we're there, but, on the other hand, these protests seem so unpatriotic. Shouldn't we be supporting what the government decided to do? Some say 'love it or leave it' about our country."

Connie shook her head firmly. "My parents always raised me to question things, not blindly follow what people say. If they're doing the right thing, we should support them, but if they're not, we need to let them know how we feel."

"You've always been one of those liberal people, Connie. I can't be like that. I like things to stay the same, no upsetting the applecart, or whatever they say," Molly said.

Martha Ann looked from one friend to the other. *And where do I stand? I guess I'm right in the middle of both of them.* "Lord, what a year this has been! Look at all the things that have happened since Christmas vacation. Sometimes, I wonder what's happening to our country."

"I know," replied Connie. "Have you had any demonstrations at the university? We didn't really at Auburn."

"Nothing like at Columbia University in New York City. That was crazy. Over seven hundred students arrested. What's that going to do to their school records?"

Molly took out a cigarette and lit it. "And what about all the riots after they killed that Martin Luther King? I was worrying that our whole country was going to be burned and looted."

"Well," began Connie, "his murder was a terrible thing. He was a great leader for the Negroes."

"Sure, but why did the Negroes get so violent?"

"I read about that. I think it was 'cause after he was killed, some went around asking businesses to close out of respect for King, and when they didn't, it made them mad, and they broke windows and started looting. Then all the Negroes thought about how mad and frustrated they were and the rioting seemed like a good idea to them, I guess," explained Connie.

"Things like that sure don't help their cause any. It was scary, I thought." Martha Ann shivered, remembering the worry that Negro violence would come to her personally. "Someone told me that they had so many National Guard units called out 'round the country that it was the most domestic troops deployed since the Civil War."

"I know that King was a real spokesman for the race stuff, but why'd he have to go and start speaking against the war in Vietnam? Why didn't he stick to civil rights?" asked Molly.

Again, Connie tried to explain. "I think it's 'cause there's so many Negroes fighting in Vietnam."

"That whole Vietnam mess, now that's another crazy thing going on," said Martha Ann.

"'Member the Tet Offensive business? All those cities attacked over there in January. We're losing so many of our men in a country nobody knows or cares about. No wonder there's so many protests going on in the United States. What are we doing over there anyway?"

"Who knows?" Molly shrugged as she kept one hand on the steering wheel and the other on her cigarette.

Connie nodded. "There's so many kinds of protesting. Did y'all hear about that play, *Hair*? I like some of the music from it, that song 'Aquarius,' but I'd never go see it. They come out naked in one part, you know."

"Naked!" exclaimed Martha Ann. "How can they dare to do that?"

"I don't know, but they do. Not only that, but John Lennon and Yoko Ono appeared naked on their album cover."

"Lord have mercy," Molly said. "What is this world coming to?"

"Let's talk about what's really important," urged Martha Ann. "Do y'all know any boys who'll be at the beach this week?"

The sound of their laughter floated out the open windows

as the car sped down the highway toward the beach.

PART TWO

ADULT YEARS

CHAPTER SIXTEEN

It is the set of our sails, not the direction of the wind, that deter-
mines which way we will go.
Jim Rohn, motivational speaker

July 1970
LETITIA

Our house has taken on that smell, that smell of medicine and
mustiness. Mama probably doesn't notice it because she's always
inside, sitting with Daddy or fixing something for him, trying
to get him to eat. I notice it, though, every time I step through
the door from the freshness of outside. And every time it makes
me want to cry. But we do have good times with Daddy, times to
talk about things we've done together, funny things, sad things. I
wouldn't give up these moments for anything.

"Lettie, honey," he said to me not long ago, "I'm so proud of
you. You graduated from the college, and you gonna be a teacher.
And you gonna marry that fine young man. I can go to Jesus,
knowing you gonna be OK."

"Oh, Daddy, don't talk about going to Jesus. I want you to
be here with us." I could hardly speak past the lump in my throat.

With his arms lying weakly by his side, he still managed
to pat my hand. "Now, don't you cry, baby girl. It's my time. My
time." He was quiet for a moment, his eyes seeming to look at
something way past me. "You did a good thing, marching for the
Movement, a real good thing. I know that now. But don't let one
bad man's doings hurt you for the rest of your life. Don't you stay
angry at the world, sugar. There's a whole passel of good folk out

149

there. If your anger builds a fence 'round you, he wins. He wins."
That seemed to take all his energy. His eyelids fluttered closed,
but he kept my hand in his. I put my other hand on my locket
and knew that Mama Lucy was talking to me through my daddy.
I wanted to argue with them, tell them it's not only one man. My
anger wasn't just because of Bull Connor's order to turn on the
hoses those years ago. It's knowing there's still so many places I'm
not welcome because of my skin color, so many attitudes that I'm
not as good as a white person. I see it in people's eyes, their body
language. It's a part of everyday life here—my life, our life.

Mae tells me that if I expect to see that, I will. Maybe so.
She's going off to law school in a few weeks. I wonder if her attitude will change then. We'll see. She and I have such a different
way of looking at everything, but that's OK. We'll be close friends
the rest of our lives. I know it.

I wake up slowly knowing I don't want today to come. Etta sleeps
in Sam's old room now, but she comes through the door and sits
on my bed. She's crying already, and now my tears join hers.

"How can we get through Daddy's funeral?" she sobs
against me.

"I don't know. I can't believe we won't ever see him again." I
reach for my locket for comfort.

"Maybe Daddy and Mama Lucy are together again. That's
what we're supposed to believe." Etta raises her tearstained face to
me, and I want to give her hope but right now, I'm only thinking
about how much I'll miss him. We sit quietly together thinking
our sad thoughts. Poor Daddy. These last few years had been so
hard for him because of the diabetes. This last time, he didn't
even know what hit him at the very end, that final stroke. But,
before that, we could see him slowly sinking away, getting weaker
and weaker.

"Come on," I finally say. "We've got to get dressed and help
Mama."

The sun's rays burn the top of my head, and the heat makes

me feel like I have to work for every breath, but I don't care about any of that. Anthony, my fiancé, is waiting for me at the entrance to St. John's, and I don't think I've ever been so glad to have his solid strength to lean on. We go in behind Mama, Etta, and Sam. I hardly notice Sam's limp anymore. We walk to Daddy's casket up by the altar. I wonder how Mama can get through this moment, but, of course, she does. We pause behind her as she gazes at Daddy, gently puts her fingers to his face, then grips Sam's arm firmly and goes to sit in the first pew. Anthony stands with Etta and me as we try to say good-bye. It looks like Daddy, but not really. He seems so much smaller and frailer than he did in life. His navy tie lies perfectly straight against the white shirt, his blue suit neat and formal looking.

After the funeral, we all go back to the house. Even though I finished college and have a job teaching at Wilson Elementary School starting in a few weeks, I'll be living here at home with Mama and Etta until Anthony and I get married in October. Sam's been on his own for several years now.

Everybody's at the house—aunts, uncles, cousins, neighbors, church friends, people Daddy worked with at the mill—all crowded into the rooms, the porch, the yard. There are plates of food everywhere, just like after Mama Lucy's funeral. The noise of conversation vibrates all around like a million butterfly wings. I hear snatches of conversations—"her fifth baby," "and then he said," "umhmm, breast cancer," "remember that?"—until it makes me dizzy.

Anthony comes up beside me and hands me a glass of iced tea. "Mae says for us to cross the street and sit on her front steps for a little," he says, nodding toward the front door. As Anthony and I start to slip out, I give Mae a quick wave of thanks.

"Just what I need." I feel better already. I take a quick, guilty glance at Mama, but she seems to be OK with Sam on one side and Etta on the other. Anthony and I ease our way through the crowd.

We sit quietly for a while. I'm feeling so bad, losing Daddy.

TURNER

Two of the most important people in my life, Daddy and Mama Lucy, are gone now. Anthony's on the step above me so I can lean on him. I think about when I met Anthony at Miles College. He was organizing a candlelight vigil when Dr. King got killed. I smile up at him now, remembering that our first few dates ended up in arguments. He was like Mae, wanting to push the envelope, do more and more for the Movement until something changed. After he graduated with his engineering degree, he went into business with his uncle and brothers. They want to have an engineering consulting business, but they do mostly construction projects now.

"I'm so sad about losing my daddy," I tell him. "But it's even more than that. This brings up all the grief from when Mama Lucy died. It's like the funerals are connected."

His hand is gently rubbing my shoulder. "I'm sure it's that way. This is a hard day for your mom, for all of you."

I nod, and my eyes tear up. "But I think the harder days are what's coming, trying to go on without him. Still, Daddy was careful about money and insurance and all, and Mama still works one day a week for that Miz Pierce."

Anthony gives me a funny look. "When you say that name, you always scowl. What did that lady do to you that makes you dislike her so much?"

"Humph. For one thing, she was always wanting Mama to bring me back to help her. That way she'd get two workers for the price of one. Or maybe she thought she was doing some kind of mission work by paying me fifty cents an hour."

"Lettie."

"Well, not only that. That girl of hers was only a little older than I am. Mama had to call her 'MISS Martha Ann.' I bet she never called my mama MIZ Robinson. No. Umhmm."

"Well, we don't need to even be talking about that family, do we, honey?"

I sigh. "'Course we don't. It's Mama we should be thinking about."

"Yeah," he agrees. "But your mama is strong."

"She is. And Etta will be at home for a few more years. I'm glad I'll be there too for a little while."

"Do you think we should postpone the wedding?"

I laugh, but it's choked with tears. "Daddy said that we were to go on with the wedding no matter when he passed. He made me promise. Said he'd come back and haunt us if we didn't." At the last words, I can't hold back the tears anymore, and I bury my face against Anthony's side.

The weeks fly by until school starts. I've been up all hours the weeks before, preparing things for my classroom—my very own classroom. Finally, it's the first day of classes. My school is over in Bessemer, and even though it's a little drive for me, I'm glad to have the job. Mainly I'm glad because Wilson is a black school. I want to be a teacher of black kids, to be sure they're getting the education they need.

The teacher in the next room, Yvonne Griggs, has been teaching for years, and she's been a big help to me already. She sticks her head into my room. "Now, you let me know if I can help you in any way, hear?"

I smile. "I hear, Miz Griggs, and thanks."

She waves a hand and disappears from view. I take a deep breath, put my hand to my locket, and I'm ready.

The children burst in from the bus lines, eager, neatly dressed for this first day.

August 1971
MARTHA ANN

Martha Ann and her fiancé, Bill Reynolds, plopped onto the bench under the shadow of Vulcan, the fifty-six-foot-tall cast-iron statue of the god of fire atop Red Mountain, the prize-winning remainder from the 1904 St. Louis World's Fair, Birmingham's tribute to its blast furnaces. The day was muggy, and both Bill and Martha Ann were flushed from their hike up the mountain.

Martha Ann took the thermos of cold tea from her pack and poured them each a cup. She sighed. "Bill, what are we gonna do? I've got my résumé out to all the school systems, but still no offers."

Bill sat forward, hands on his knees. "I don't know. Until I'm earning a decent salary, there's no way we can afford to get married."

Martha Ann frowned. "I know."

"You'd be a good teacher, honey. Someone'll hire you."

"I think I would be too, but I keep hearing the same thing—they give the Vietnam vets first consideration for jobs. Taking substitute jobs won't earn me enough for us to live on." They sat quietly for a moment, gazing out over the city of Birmingham. The leaves of the tall trees around them occasionally rustled, but there wasn't much of a breeze. Martha Ann turned to her fiancé. "Bill, do you really still want to marry me? You're not stalling to get out of it, are you?"

Bill leaned his head back, his blond hair brushing the bench top, as he laughed. "No, my darling Martha Ann, I am not trying to weasel out a' marrying you. But until I'm through with my master's degree, if you don't have a full-time teaching job, we simply can't afford it."

Martha Ann frowned. "But what if I never get a job? I'm so discouraged."

Bill patted her leg. "Now, hon, we can't stew about that now. Something is sure to turn up."

Martha Ann shook her head. "I hope so. It's getting awful close to the school year starting. And I surely am tired of living in my parents' home."

He pulled her close and kissed her. "We'll keep on hoping and praying. That's all we can do."

The call came a week later. When Martha Ann answered the phone, she was surprised to hear the voice of Robert Graham, the superintendent at Bessemer and a church acquaintance. After some casual conversation, he got right to the point. "Martha Ann, I have an opening for a fourth-grade teacher. Are you interested?"

She felt her breath catch in her throat and her heart skip a beat. "Am I interested? You bet. That's wonderful."

He paused a moment. "Before you say yes, I need to tell you that the position is at Wilson School."

"Wilson? I'm not sure I know that school."

"It's in Bessemer. Right now, it's a black school."

"A black school?" Martha Ann knew she shouldn't sound so surprised.

"Well, they're trying to have it be integrated, but it's a neighborhood school, and it's right in the middle of a black neighborhood."

The racing of Martha Ann's heart was even stronger. What should she say? She desperately needed the job. But a black school? "Uh, how many white teachers are there?" she asked.

Robert Graham cleared his throat. "Right now there aren't any. But, Martha Ann, I'm sure we'll be getting some in the future."

"In the future?" She seemed to be repeating everything he said.

"Yes. This is the only opening right now, though. The teacher we had has had to drop out for health reasons. I knew you were looking for a teaching position, so thought I'd offer it to you first. What do you think?"

"Well, I . . . I mean, uh, how soon do you need an answer? Could I talk to my fiancé about it and get back to you tomorrow?"

"Sure. I think that would be all right. But I will need an answer tomorrow, one way or another."

"Of course. I understand. And, Mr. Graham, I really do appreciate your thinking of me. I surely do."

They ended the conversation, and Martha Ann sank down in the kitchen chair. *Oh, my God, a black school. Whatever should I do?*

She turned to her mother, who came into the kitchen at that moment.

"Was that for you, sugar?" her mother asked.

Martha Ann nodded. "Mom, that was Robert Graham. You know, from church? He offered me a job."

"That's wonderful! I know you're relieved."

"Mom, it's at a black school."

Her mother looked at her, her hand covering her mouth. "A black school?"

"Umhmm."

"Oh, your father won't like that. Not at all."

Martha Ann stood up quickly. "Mom, it doesn't matter what Daddy thinks. This is my life. I'll decide."

"He'll forbid it."

"How can he forbid me to do anything? I'm a grown woman. Bill and I will decide." Martha Ann stormed out of the room. *Daddy has always run my life by his racist thinking. No more! I'll take this job. That'll show him he can't control me anymore.*

There wasn't much time to prepare her first classroom, and besides, there was a wedding date to set. They decided on December 20. In the meantime, Martha Ann worked in a flurry of activity to set up the classroom. Her father wasn't speaking to her after their argument about taking the job. *I don't care what Daddy thinks. I need this job so Bill and I can get married. That matters more than anything Daddy might say.*

At school the other teachers, all black, had greeted her politely, but nothing more—no offers to help, no friendly chats getting to know each other, but, at least, no obvious hostility.

The first day of school, Martha Ann dressed carefully in a neat navy shirtwaist dress and navy pumps. Her room was in readiness for the students, and she stood at the door greeting them as they arrived, feeling a strange uneasiness and nervousness. "Hello, Tamika, Marcus, DeAndre. Welcome Jazmine, Anna, Darius." And she thought, *How am I ever going to remember these names? And the way they look at me, like I'm someone from another planet. Did I make a mistake taking this job?*

The morning went smoothly, and Martha Ann was pleased with her class and her lesson plan. The children seemed eager to learn and were responsive to her. She began to relax. One boy in particular, James, reminded her so much of Brad at that age. His desk was already a hodgepodge of papers, all with drawings on them, and several paper airplanes had found their way to the trash basket.

Immediately after lunch the principal stuck his head in to see how she was doing. Mr. Harris was the one person who had made her feel comfortable, who seemed to be supportive of her. She knew from her student-teaching days that the attitude of the principal was so important in how a teacher liked the school, and in whether or not a teacher could succeed. He did not seem to put any barriers between them simply because he was black and she was white.

At the end of the day Martha Ann straightened up the classroom and laid out the books and papers she would need for tomorrow. Stopping at the doorway, she paused and looked back. She smiled, flicked off the light, and headed home, feeling very good about her first day as a real teacher.

CHAPTER SEVENTEEN

It [the cause of improved race relations] is a matter of developing a sense of trust based on everybody—black and white—trying to start from the same place. That is admittedly harder for blacks to do than whites... But there must come a time in the life of every community... when we must recognize that we are all in this together—when we must move past the old divisions of race and recognize our common interests and our common humanity.

William Winter, former Mississippi governor, *speech, Jackson, Mississippi, March 1, 1999*

Fall 1971
LETITIA

We're into a new school year, and already I'm loving it. My class has more boys than girls, and that's always a challenge. But there's something about the boys that reminds me of Sam when he was a kid, so I think I enjoy them more. Some of the kids are so eager to learn. When I see them respond to my teaching, I know exactly why I wanted to be a teacher. *Mama Lucy, take a look at where I am.* I chuckle to myself as I touch my cherished locket.

This afternoon, Yvonne Griggs and I are the only ones in the teachers' lounge. She passes me a chocolate-chip cookie from the plate of goodies she brought today. "How's everything going, Letitia? Is your second year going to be as good as last year was?"

I swallow my bite of cookie. "Fine, I think. I really like my students. Of course, I have to admit that things don't always go like my lesson plan says they should." We both smile at that.

Yvonne is my favorite of all the teachers. Seems like she

always has a smile and is ready to help when you need it. During last year Yvonne and I really got to know each other well enough to use our first names. That's a big step because everyone is so formal in this adult world.

"Can I ask you a personal question?" she asks. I'm caught by surprise. I wouldn't expect that but we've become friendly enough so I don't mind a personal question from her.

"Sure."

"Well, I can't help but wonder. That new white teacher, Martha Ann Pierce?"

I tense up but nod my head.

"I can tell you don't like her. I'm only wondering. Not my business, I know. Did she do something to offend you?"

I grit my teeth. Should I say anything? Finally, I let my breath out in a big sigh.

"Not really," I admit, "but my mother works for her mother and has for years and years."

"Oh, so y'all know each other."

"No. In all the years, I only saw her one time, and that was at her sixteenth birthday party. When she started here, I recognized her name, but she wouldn't have known my married name. I was so afraid she'd know me for some reason and say something like, 'Oh, are you that po' little colored girl I'd give my old clothes to?' or 'Oh, you're Willa's daughter that was washin' dishes for my birthday party.'"

Yvonne hoots her throaty laugh. "Girl, you are a case."

I feel a little hurt at Yvonne's reaction. I thought she'd see my side.

"Look, Letitia," she says, patting my arm. "It's a big world out there, and we got to make our way the best we can. It doesn't do any good to hold grudges, especially the imagined kind. That Miss Pierce doesn't know a thing about you, so let it go. Anyway, she's like a little lost lamb here."

I look at Yvonne and see Mae and Mama Lucy in her all at once. I put my hand to my locket. There really is no way Martha

Ann Pierce would know me. Maybe I can let go of that worry. I grin. "You're right. Miss Pierce is kinda lost here since she's the only white teacher."

Yvonne nods. "Why, honey, she brings her lunch every day and sits in the ladies room for us teachers and eats all by herself. One time I told her come eat with us, but she said everyone, including herself, was probably more comfortable that way. I hear she's getting married in December."

"I'll have to learn her new last name," I say.

"I believe it's a common name. Let me think." She closes her eyes for a moment. "I've got it, it's Reynolds. Her name will be Miz Reynolds."

All day I've been bursting with news, but I couldn't say anything until this afternoon's doctor's appointment. Now that the doctor has given me the official word that I'm pregnant, I can't wait to get home and tell Anthony. I know Anthony won't be there for a while, but I still want to rush home. Our timing is perfect. I can have the baby during the summer and be ready to teach in the fall again.

I hear Anthony open the door and come in with his usual call: "I'm home." I can't wait to tell him. I walk in the den. He'll click on the news after a quick kiss, I know.

He looks at me. "And what are you smiling about? You look like the cat that swallowed the canary."

I'd planned to at least let him sit down first, but there's no holding back. I walk over and take his hand in mine. "Anthony, I'm pregnant. We're going to have a baby."

His face breaks out in that big smile I love so much, and he hugs me to him. "That's great news, baby. I'm so happy." He pulls back and looks at me, a mischievous smile curling up his lips. "It didn't take long once we decided to try, did it? I must be the man, right, girl? I'm the man." He struts around the room, chanting "I'm the man. I'm the man."

I have to laugh.

TURNER

After dinner I curl up on the couch next to Anthony while he watches TV. He puts his arm 'round me and kisses the top of my head the way I like.

"We are lucky folk, Letitia. A beautiful baby on the way."

"Well, we don't know if it'll be a daughter or a son. Are you hoping for a boy?"

"You know, it doesn't make a bit of difference to me."

"I'm glad," I say as I snuggle in closer.

"And now that my business is doing so well, you won't have to go back to work after this baby."

I sit up straight. "What are you talking about? Not go back to work?"

He turns toward me, a puzzled look on his face. "But don't you want to stay home with our kids, Letitia?"

"Well, at first, but I don't want to stop teaching."

He shakes his head. "I thought if you had the choice, you'd stay home, quit teaching."

"Why would you ever think that? I'm a teacher. You know I'm a teacher. That's not only what I do, that's who I am. Ever since the Movement, I've worked for that, been determined to do that."

Anthony gets up and turns off the TV then comes back and sits next to me. He takes my hand in his, and the look on his face tells me this is important. "Lettie, I know how you feel about the Movement and all that happened with it. I understand about your anger and your drive to do your part to make things better for blacks. But think about this. You'd be making things better for our own precious child if you'd quit work and stay home. I make a good living for us now. I can provide what we need so you can do that."

I feel myself bristling; I can't help it. I take my hand from his and shake my finger in his face. "Now you listen to me, Anthony Williams, and you listen good. I can take care of any children, and this house, and you perfectly well and still be a teacher. If I gave up teaching, why I . . . I . . . I don't know. I'd feel like I was nothing. Nothing. We got to educate our young ones, and we got to have teachers to do that. And that's what I do, and what I'm going to keep on doing. You hear me?" By now, my voice is really loud and the tears are starting, so I jump off the couch and run to our bedroom. I throw myself across the bed and give in to my tears.

Pretty soon Anthony comes in, like I knew he would. He sits on the edge of the bed. I hear him sigh, and he starts rubbing my back.

"Letitia, honey, if that's the way you feel, then that's the way it'll be."

I try to stop my sniffling and turn to face him. "You'll be OK with my teaching?"

"Looks like I don't have a choice, do I?" He smiles as he says it, so I know he's not too mad or disappointed.

I smile back at him and swing my legs over the side so I can sit up next to him. "Anthony," I begin, wanting to explain myself to him. "Being a teacher is all tied up with being black for me. It's kind of like we feel when we watch about Dr. King or George Washington Carver or Sojourner Truth, you know? Remember how we felt when we thought about our backgrounds, our connection to strong black people?"

Anthony nods his head, but I can see he doesn't get the connection I'm trying to make. "Well, it's like who we are is so tied to who we were and who we came from."

"Yeah, I get that part."

"It's like that for me. The Movement was so important to me. It connects who I was, a kid made so angry by discrimination, to who I am today, an adult who wants to see all black kids get ahead, have a fair chance at life. To do that, I have to be a teacher. My folks worked so hard for me to get an education so I could teach. I can't let them down. Don't you see?"

He gets that mischievous smile again. "Sure, honey, I see. And here I thought it was only your crazy hormones acting up."

I swat his shoulder on that. He laughs and pushes me back

on the bed, starting to kiss me. I stop thinking about anything else.

Fall 1971
MARTHA ANN

Sitting by Bill on the living room sofa, Martha Ann slowly turned the pages of *Brides Magazine*. "Which bouquet do you like better, this one or that one?" she asked, flipping the pages from one picture to another. *The plans for the wedding are coming along so well. Why can't I decide about flowers?* The church was reserved for an afternoon wedding with the reception in the fellowship hall; her dress was selected and was getting its final alteration. Still, she couldn't figure out what to do about the flowers.

Bill looked at the pictures, then at Martha Ann. "They're both pretty. I don't know anything about flowers. Whatever you want is fine with me."

She put down the magazine and sighed. "I want our wedding to be perfect, Bill."

He leaned over and kissed her. "It'll be perfect, don't worry." He turned his attention back to the football game on TV.

"Well, a lot depends on my daddy, of course. He could spoil everything by keeping his grumpy attitude. Mom's getting him to come 'round, but he's still so mad at me about taking that job at a black school."

"I think he'll be fine, Martha Ann. He wants what's best for you, that's all."

She sighed again. "I know. And, I have to admit, the first few days of school, I wondered if he'd been right."

"I know you had a shaky start, but it's OK now, isn't it?" he asked, momentarily taking his gaze off the game.

"Oh, yeah. Now, only a few short months into the school year, everything's different. The kids are my kids now, and things are going along fine. I'm truly enjoying the class." *Well, maybe not everything's so fine.* She'd been shocked at the dilapidated condition of the school and supplies. The books weren't the shiny new ones she was used to in the white schools. When she expressed her dismay to the other teachers, they looked at her with a strange expression, almost as if it were her fault, as if anyone white was responsible for all injustices by whites. At least, that's how their expressions made Martha Ann feel. When she walked into the teachers' lounge, conversations became subdued and joking stopped. She was definitely an outsider and was likely to remain so. Only Mr. Harris, the black principal, made her feel that she was one of them, part of the faculty. Her time with the students and the evenings were her favorite times of the day.

Bill looked at her, took her hand in his. "Are you sorry you took this job, honey?"

"Oh, no," she replied quickly. "My kids are great." She smiled to herself when she realized her first response was to affirm the job. "And, besides, now we can get married. That's the most important thing." But then she sighed. "It's only that, oh, I don't know. I can't help it, but I kind of feel lonely in my job. That's why I joined that book club, and started singing in the choir, so I could have time with friends. It makes me sad, but I know the black teachers will never be friends with me. They don't want to."

Bill looked at her for a long moment. "And you? Do you want to be friends with them?"

PART THREE

THE TORNADO

CHAPTER EIGHTEEN

Courage is resistance to fear, mastery of fear, not absence of fear.
Mark Twain

April 17, 1975, 3:30 p.m.
THE TORNADO

Black. Everything's black. Am I dead?
Take a deep breath. God, that hurts. Calm down. Think.
The tornado. I remember now. The tornado was coming right
at the school. The children! Oh, yeah, thank God they're all gone.
Just some of us teachers still here. That blackness filled the sky. The
noise, oh God, I could feel the noise in my bones. That swirling gray
in front of the blackness, spewing all kinds of things. Everything was
shaking, like an earthquake. Where am I? Oh, I remember run-
ning to the teachers' lounge in the center of the building. Like they
always say to do. Someone was running behind me? Yvonne? Mr.
Mills? That white teacher? Who was it?
Why is it so dark? Can I move? My head and neck seem OK,
but I can't turn. Smoke. It's so hard to breathe. No, not smoke, dust.
Everything must have collapsed around me. Oh, God, am I going to
die? Help me. Please help me! Get me out of here. How long have I
been trapped here? I must have been knocked out, but for how long?
I can't tell if it's day or night.
"Help! Is anyone there? Can anyone hear me?"
Oh, Lord, Lord, help me. Mama always says you walk with
us. Where are you? I don't want to die. Anthony and I have such a
good life with our daughter. My daughter! Felicia! I can't die. We've

*got so many plans, Lord. Don't let this happen. Help—someone—
find me. That smell. Like when lightning strikes close by. Ozone?*
"Help! Help, anyone!"
*What's happened to everyone else? I know Yvonne was still
here, and Mr. Mills, and that white teacher, Miz Reynolds. Did they
get away? Are they hurt? Oh, Lord, Lord, I'm scared. Calm. I know
I gotta stay calm. Deep breaths.*
That's better.
*But where was this tornado headed? Are Felicia and Anthony
OK? Felicia would have been at day care. Yes, they'd be down in
the basement. When I looked out and saw the tornado coming, it
wasn't from that direction. I'm sure. Am I sure? Oh, please let her be
safe! Don't let her be afraid. And Anthony? He was working out in
Hoover today, he said. Yeah, the other direction.*
*That awful noise has stopped. I've never heard a noise like
that, so loud it was crushing me. Like a freight train; like ten freight
trains at once. The dust is settling. It's not really night after all,
there's still light. If I could only twist around a little, I could see my
watch. There. Oh, it's 3:40. I guess I wasn't really unconscious.*
*Maybe if I can brace my arms under me, I can roll over. I
don't feel like anything is broken, but my heart feels like it's going
to jump out of my chest. Will I die of a heart attack? Stop it! Calm
down. We're a surviving people, Mama always tells us. We've got to
be smart. That's all I've got to do.*
"Help! I'm down here. Is anyone there?"
*The ringing in my ears is stopping, but now it's so quiet.
So still. Am I the only one left alive? Oh, God! Anthony! Felicia!
Mama!*
*I'm thirsty. My mouth tastes of dust and grit. My chest hurts.
If I could sit up, but is this part of the ceiling on top of me? No, I
remember. I dove under the big table in the teachers' lounge. I can
move a little, but I can't get out from under all this, this, whatever's
fallen down on top of me.*
"Help! Somebody, please help me!"
My heart is racing, and I feel like I'm being crushed. That's

bringing up a horrible memory of something. What? What is it that is making me even more scared? It's . . . it's what? I can't think. The darkness, the water, the terror, what is it?

I don't want to be all alone here. Am I the only one left alive? Oh, Jesus, Jesus, I am so scared. Why is this happening? I don't want to be trapped and alone when it gets dark. Please, I'm praying with all a' my soul, Jesus. Wait—was that a noise?

"Hello! Is someone here?"

I can hear a moan. It sounds close, but I still can barely see anything beyond all this pile of rubble.

"Who's there? Are you hurt?"

"Oh h h."

"Who is that? Yvonne? Is that you, Yvonne?"

"No. It's . . . Martha Ann . . . Martha . . ."

"Martha Ann Reynolds? Keep talking so I know where you are."

"My . . . my leg. My leg is trapped. I can't . . . move."

"You're close, but I can hardly move either. I think you're near my right side. I'll try to get closer. Hang on. Try to hang on."

Maybe if I push myself this way. Yes, I can edge closer. I wish there wasn't all this debris piled around me. Lord, help me do this. You got to be with me now, Lord.

"Miz Reynolds. Can you hear me?"

"Oh h. Yes . . . I . . ."

"I'm moving closer. I can inch my way toward your voice."

"My leg."

"I know. But we're alive. We'll get out. We're not alone."

Alone. Oh, Lord, thank you that I'm not by myself down here. But what happened to the others? Did they get out? They were down the hall from us. Oh, God, please let them be all right. They knew we were here. If they got out, maybe they've gone for help.

"Miz Reynolds. Talk to me. I'm trying to get closer. Is it only your leg that's trapped?"

"My leg. Oh, God. But I . . . I hear you close."

She sounds so near. Why can't I see her yet? It's dust. So much dust in the air. I can get a little closer, though. Yes! I can see her! I'm not alone!

"I see you. I can see you now. We'll be OK. We'll get out somehow. Don't cry. Don't cry now."

"Tears of . . . joy that . . . I'm not . . . alone. Who . . . ?"

"It's Letitia. Letitia Williams."

The dust is settling. I can see some shards of light coming through. I can see her now, the white teacher. The dust that's settled on her makes her look even whiter. I wonder if I look white too. Thank you, Jesus, that we're together in this, that we're not alone. We barely spoke in school, but now—

"Miz Williams. The tornado?"

"Yes, that tornado was coming right at us. I saw how black the sky was, then it covered us. I ran, ran for the teachers' lounge. Everything collapsed around us. I think I got knocked out for a moment, maybe not. I don't know. It's such a confusing blur. I'm OK, but I'm afraid to move."

"The others? I know someone else was here."

"I hope they got out. It was Yvonne Griggs and Mr. Mills. They're probably getting help for us. Can you move at all?"

"No. The rest of me is OK, not hurt, but I'm stuck like this, on my side. Can you move? Can you get help?"

"I can shift around, but not much."

"How can we get out of here? What'll we do?"

"Someone will come, Miz Reynolds. I'm sure someone will come. We need to stay calm, keep talking. We can do this."

"I . . . I don't know."

"Don't talk like that. Think about your family. Do you have any kids?"

"Jason. We have a boy, Jason."

I remember then that she'd been pregnant and taken maternity leave a couple of years ago. Funny, I'd never asked about the baby after she came back.

"We've got a girl, Felicia. Me and my husband, Anthony."

"Mine. Bill."

Oh, my God. What's happened to Anthony and Felicia? Oh, my Jesus, please keep them safe. I need to know they're OK. I have to get out of here! We need to keep talking, keep our minds off that we're trapped here. I'm so scared. I can hear the wind and rain now, but it's getting lighter. That terrible darkness, the water, the noise. like some evil thing surrounding us. What is it reminding me of? I can't think about that. We have to keep talking.

"How old is Jason?" I ask.

"He's sixteen months old. He's beautiful, blond like his daddy. Yours?"

"Felicia's three."

We're quiet for a few moments. It's hard to think about having a conversation, but I guess Miz Reynolds knows that's important too, 'cause she starts to say something.

"Did you grow up in Birmingham, Miz Williams?"

I pause. In the last two years, I'd almost forgotten that Mama worked for her mother. Should I tell her now? If I do, she'll know I'm the one she sent her clothes to. Can I stand her knowing?

"Miz Williams?" Her voice carries a note of panic. "Are you there?"

"Yeah, I'm here. I'll move more so you can see me. We have to keep calm."

"I know. I'll try. It helps if we keep talking. I graduated from Shades Valley High School. What about you? Did you grow up here?"

The thought slips quickly through my mind that maybe God put us here together to clear the air about this. "Miz Reynolds," I say finally. "My mother worked for your mother until last year."

"Your mother? You mean Willa is your mother?"

"Umhmm. Willa Robinson."

"Well, why didn't you ever say anything? Willa was such a big help to my mom, and she was always so nice to me and Brad. What a small world."

I am amazed that this is finally out in the open. It almost feels like a relief. "I graduated from Parker High School," I tell her, hoping to leave the other subject behind.

"We were just over the mountain. But back then, it might as well have been in a different country, right?" she says. I move a little so we're facing each other now. Still, I can't quite meet her gaze.

I want to say *"boy, that's the truth; you didn't know we existed,"* but I hold my tongue. "Yes. That was such a . . . such a different time." I put my hand to my throat, relieved to find my locket still there. *Mama Lucy, I hope you and Daddy are watching over me and will get me out of this. I know you're smiling about me stuck here with this white person, of all the people in the world. If we get out of here OK, I don't care that we're trapped together. At least I'm not alone.*

CHAPTER NINETEEN

I have learned that lessons find us wherever we may be,
if we listen we may discover what we believe.
Doann Houghton-Alico, *"What I Have Learned," Dancing Fish*

3:55 p.m.

The tornado has passed on, but there is still wind and rain. I can hear it beating on what's left of our school. I can see shafts of light through the massive slabs of the building piled around me. *Why? Why did this happen to me?* I know there's no answer.

At least now the dust has settled and the blackness has passed over so I can see. *Lord, I pray you're sending someone to find us.*

"Miz Reynolds, we need to keep talking to each other. I can see now that it was that big table in the teachers' lounge that saved us. It kept a lot of the ceiling from falling on us. I think I can move around a little."

"Be careful. Something might shift."

"Don't worry, I'll be very careful. I can lift up a little by leaning on my elbow so I can see you. Oh, I see a beam across your leg."

"Can you move it off of me, Miz Williams?"

"No. I can't move that much."

"Oh, God, I don't want to die here!"

"You're not going to die, Miz Reynolds. They'll be digging for us soon. I'm sure of it."

"How can you be such an optimist?"

I give a little grunt. I don't think anyone's ever called me an optimist. Maybe when I was young, before the Movement. I can pinpoint that time when I learned to stay strong, when we all learned to be strong. The Movement. "I'm no optimist but I know that we've got to stay strong. That was the most important lesson I learned from the . . . from life."

Miz Reynolds keeps that steady gaze on me. "What were you going to say, Miz Williams? From the what?"

I shift my position a little to avoid those blue eyes. Should I answer? Finally, I say, "From the Movement."

"The Movement?"

"You know. Back in the '60s. Do you remember when Dr. King was here? It was this time of year." Suddenly, I realize what this tornado reminds me of, that terrible time of Bull Connor's turning the hoses on us, the pressure of the water, the difficulty getting my breath. It all comes back to me in a flash. I feel sick to my stomach, bile rising in my throat.

"Do you mean when all the children marched and got arrested?"

"Uh huh."

"Did you march, Miz Williams?"

"My brother Sam and I both marched. He got arrested, and they kept him for twelve days."

Miz Reynolds is quiet for a few moments, then asks, "You didn't get arrested?"

"No. I got hosed."

"Yes, I remember. My daddy wouldn't let us go downtown. I read about the fire hoses. My God, that was so awful."

"You can't even imagine; it was an awful time." *This white person does not even have a clue what it was like.*

Miz Reynolds closes her eyes. Silence settles around us. We can hear sirens in the distance, the spattering of rain somewhere overhead.

"I didn't really understand what the demonstrations were

for, what you hoped to achieve. I . . . I've never talked to a black person about it."

I almost smile. "I've never talked to a white person about it either," I have to answer. I can't help but wonder how many blacks and whites have ever talked about it to each other. Not many, I bet. "How's your leg now?"

"It hurts some. It's better if I lie absolutely still. But you didn't answer me. I did wonder about the protests when all that was going on."

I try not to look at her like she's crazy. Why are we discussing this? Does she really want to know? How can I explain to a white person what it felt like growing up black in Birmingham in those years? Surely, they know the facts; that there were lynchings, bombings, beatings, harassment, all the results of so many years of discrimination, bigotry, and hate. But there's no way they can know the feelings, the fear, the confusion when you see the adults you respect grovel away their dignity in front of some white person, the anger when you learn your limitations—where you can't go, what you can't do, how blacks always got the leftovers, including school books. Still, we're here now, and we need to keep talking, to survive. I nod my head and take a deep breath.

I try to tell her as honestly as I can. "We had some black leaders who had been trying for years to make changes here. Life in our own communities was secure, but we lived with fear, at least the adults did. They always were afraid that they would do something to make the whites mad, and they would lose their jobs, or their homes, or their cars would be repossessed, or even worse might happen. The Klan was definitely active, and turning to the white police force was pointless."

"But, surely, there were good white people here."

"I'm sure there were some, but our paths usually didn't cross with whites except when they were in a position of authority. How could we know who was good and who was bad? To be safe, we lumped them all together and didn't take chances."

Miz Reynolds frowns. I can see she doesn't like my answer,

but I go on.

"Finally, that spring of 1963, Rev. Shuttlesworth and Wyatt Tee Walker from the Southern Christian Leadership Conference got Dr. Martin Luther King, Jr., to come to Birmingham. They thought that by Dr. King and Ralph Abernathy preaching at the mass meetings they held at the black churches, well, they thought everyone would get fired up and march with him."

Miz Reynolds's gaze never left mine. She gave a tiny nod, so I continued.

"But that didn't happen. The adults were too scared, I guess. The civil rights movement was starting to get the news media to follow what they were doing, and the reporters had come to Birmingham, but I guess they weren't finding enough news. Dr. King had hoped to fill the jails and show how terrible life was for blacks under Bull Connor so that the nation and the federal government would pay attention, but since that wasn't happening, he decided to get himself arrested. There was an injunction against them to hold the marches, so when they did march, they were arrested for parading without a permit. Even though he and Rev. Abernathy got arrested, still that didn't get much attention. That's when he called in Rev. Bevel. He was the one that inspired all of us kids to march."

"How did he do that?"

In all the years since that time, I'd read and studied about what happened. This is the first time, though, that I've really talked about it on such a personal basis. How strange that my listener is this white person. I shake my head, lean back, and let my thoughts travel to that time. *God, we were all so young, so naïve.*

"Well, Rev. Bevel was certainly charismatic. We loved him and would have followed him anywhere. Why?" I shrug. The reason wasn't anything I could say in words. It was a power he poured into us. It was a light he radiated, a glow that we couldn't hold in our hands yet burned itself into our souls. I try to fit it into language. "We didn't know enough to be afraid like our parents were. He stirred us into believing we could change history, that we could make a better world." I bite my lip to hold back the tears that might come with remembering.

Miz Reynolds again tries to shift a little. I know she is in pain and needs our conversation to distract her. I'm about to try to explain how we felt marching, but she starts speaking as she looks away.

"I remember that time very well," she begins. "It was a time of change for everyone, I think. I was really beginning to see the world as it was, not as I'd always thought of it. My daddy, I'm sorry to say,"—she glances quickly at me, then turns away—"my daddy was such a racist. I don't think he was in the Klan, but he had the same attitudes. My mom tried to give us some balance. Still, we didn't know anything about blacks, about what life was like for you. I'd never been around a black person, ever, until I came to work here, except for your mother, of course. But she came while I was at school. I never really visited with her. There were a few when I went to college at Alabama, but they kept to themselves."

As if they had a choice. Mae had gone to the University of Alabama, and I know all about how it was, how separate the blacks stayed from the whites. I often think about how hard it had been for those first young people that were in the vanguard of integration, how lonely and isolated they must have felt, what courage it must have taken. And then the thought strikes me. *When Miz Reynolds started working here at Wilson School, she was the only white person. What was that like for her?*

We've been silent for a while, each lost in our own memories of those turbulent times, each remembering through our own lives, I guess.

Miz Reynolds breaks the silence. "Tell me about your family."

"My family?"

"Yeah. Do you have brothers or sisters?"

"I have an older brother, Sam. He joined the Marines after high school, then went to trade school. He's a plumber and lives in Bessemer. My younger sister Etta is going to be a teacher too. You?"

"Only one brother, Brad. He works for South Central Bell."

I can't help but think that we've both worked at this school for almost five years and we have never talked about our families, ourselves. We've talked about the school, the administration, compared notes on students, but never anything personal. The closest we ever got to a personal conversation was one time we were talking about what a great principal Mr. Harris is. Martha Ann mentioned that he was the reason she stayed at Wilson School even though by then she could have transferred to a white school. I remember I gave her a funny look, but we never said any more about it. Is there a hidden wall between us that holds us back from each other?

We let the quiet enfold us, but after a while it makes me uneasy. I need to say something reassuring—for both of us. "There's still a few hours before dark. Someone will come. I'm sure of it." Miz Reynolds lies with her eyes closed.

I wonder if I should let her drift asleep, or would that be dangerous. Oh, God, this is so scary. I don't know what to do. Why isn't anyone around looking for us? Anthony, I need you. Are you OK? Did the tornado head toward where you were working? Do you know that I'm still at school? And Felicia, Lord, please be watching over them.

"I'm so thirsty," Miz Reynolds says, her eyes still closed.

"Me too. I know there were things we could drink here in the teachers' lounge, but I can't get to anything."

Miz Reynolds opens her eyes and looks at me. "Tell me some more. Talk to me about your life."

"I've been talking so much. Why don't you talk?"

"My life wasn't so interesting. An average kind of life—" She pauses.

I look over at Miz Reynolds. Now she's lying there with her eyes wide open, simply staring at nothing.

"Are you OK?" I ask.

She looks my way. "Yeah, I was thinking about what you said, remembering back to those years. Those were really bad times. I was thinking about when the church was bombed and those four girls died."

I'm not sure I want to talk about the bombing so I keep quiet.

"Did you know any of those four girls?"

I look away. I think it will always hurt to remember that time. "Yes. Carole Robertson went to Parker with me."

"Was she a friend?"

"Not a close friend, but I knew her."

"Were you at the church that day?"

God, why was she pushing about this? I don't want to bring up these feelings. I don't want to remember the fog of smoke 'round the church, the smell of dynamite, the desperate calls for loved ones.

"I didn't go to that church. We go to St. John's A.M.E. Church. My family's gone there for three generations."

"Do you remember much about that time of the bombing?"

I pause a moment and bite my lower lip to try to stop the trembling. "I remember it like it was yesterday, every horrible detail."

When I turn back toward Miz Reynolds, I see that she's crying silently. I don't understand why she is so emotional about the bombing. She didn't know the girls personally. What was it to her?

I hear her take a deep breath, trying to get control again. "Do you feel like that day was a milestone, I mean like a changing point in history?"

I'd thought about that a lot myself. "Yes, I really do. I believe that the Children's March and then the killing of those girls was what got the nation's attention, and, of course, the March on Washington too. It certainly got the president and Bobby Kennedy to consider what was going on. We could never have gone forward in the civil rights movement if we hadn't finally gotten some legislation behind it."

Miz Reynolds brushes away the tears left on her face. "That's what I've come to believe too."

I feel like I have to say more. "But it's not legislation that changes people and their attitudes and fears. We've got a long way to go."

"That's true. But we were in such separate worlds. I mean, we didn't know anything about each other, and we have to understand one another, don't we, if we're to get along? I never thought of blacks as having close neighbors, strong families, having a regular life. All I had heard of blacks was protesting and demonstrating, and what awful people they were. What you thought of whites was that they caused trouble for you, made you afraid. How can any of that be a basis for friendships? How can people change the way they have thought and felt all their lives?"

4:25 p.m.

"What time is it?"

I move my arm so I can see my watch. "It's 4:25."

"It'll be dark soon. Why don't they come for us?"

"They'll come. Our husbands will know we're here. They'll come soon."

"I don't know how much longer I can lie like this. Can you move around any more?"

"A little, but I can't turn enough to see about your leg. How is it?"

"It's sort of numb, but I don't think anything's broken. It's simply stuck, and I can't move from lying almost on my side like this. I sure wish we had something to drink."

I try to shift around a little more to see if I can see anything, but there is so much debris piled around us, I really can't get my bearings. Then I remember the peppermint hard candy in my pocket. I start to mention it, but there's only one. Shall I offer it to her, or save it for myself?

I push my hair back and shift my position a little. Keep talking. We've got to keep talking. "Did you always want to be a teacher?"

"Not really. I didn't know what I wanted to be for a long time. It really worried me in high school. My mom pushed me about going to college, so I knew I had to be thinking about it." She pauses and looks so sad. It makes me wonder what she's thinking.

"Finally, I simply decided that I wanted to go to Alabama and become a teacher. To be honest, when I looked at the life my mother had—" She shakes her head. "A life without choices. You know what I mean? Anyway, I finally figured out that a career as a teacher would give me the security to stand on my own if I ever needed to. I became determined then to become a teacher."

"Are you glad you became one?"

She looks at me and pauses a minute before she answers. "Yes, I'm glad. You know, no one has ever asked me that before. I'm not sure I even considered that question myself." She frowns. "I must be the kind of person who only drifts through life, never really looking deeply at things. I was that way in school. In high school, we cared about our friends, and boys, and parties. I worked to get good grades, but only because that was what I was supposed to do. I went to church and had school spirit and all." Again, she pauses. "It's strange. I never thought much about what I was doing. I just did it."

I nod, although I'm not sure I understand what she means. *Her comments make me think about the way I've lived my life. How odd this is, that she and I, of all people, can have our words touch places so deep inside each other, make us think about things we never considered. We don't really know each other, but it feels like friends talking.*

She interrupts my thoughts with a question. "Did you always want to be a teacher, Letitia?"

The sound of my first name from her surprises me. I guess that shows on my face.

"Can I call you Letitia?" she asks. "Miz Williams sounds so formal now. Will you call me Martha Ann?"

What can I say? "OK." I pause, then answer her question, "Yes, I always did plan to teach. In fact, that was another thing that came from my participating in the Movement. I saw education as a way for blacks to progress, and if I became a teacher, why, I would be doing important work for the advancement of all blacks. After I got hosed during the Children's March I didn't ever want to be involved in the demonstrations again. Yet, I wanted, needed, to feel like I was doing something for civil rights."

"That makes sense."

"When I was in high school, everything was so intense because of what was going on with the civil rights movement. We all felt that we had to be a part of it in some way."

"But was it all so serious? Didn't you do the kinds of things we white kids did in high school?"

I can see why she wonders that. "'Course, we did. After all, we were teenagers. We had tremendous school spirit, so all the athletic events were important. We had dances and parties too. Remember, we couldn't go downtown to the Alabama Theater and have a Coke after, to Kiddieland, the state fair, things like that, so we didn't do much dating. We gathered at church or at someone's house. But friends, boys, um hmm, that's what it was all about."

She smiles at me, the last of the daylight sifting through the debris to touch her face. I'm struck by the thought that she has such a kind face, that when she smiles it carries into her eyes. I've never considered that about a white person before.

4:40

"What time is it, Letitia?"

I look at my watch again. "Almost 4:40." *Lord, when will someone come? Can't they see this school crumbled? Sure, they knew*

*the kids were gone, but don't they think some of us teachers might
still be here? Does this mean that Yvonne and Mr. Mills haven't gone
for help? What's happened to them? Oh, sweet Jesus, I can't think
about that or I'll panic. I've got to keep strong. I've got to!*

"Martha Ann,"—saying the name seems so strange—"keep
talking to me. Tell me what your husband's like. How did y'all
meet?"

"Bill?" She takes a deep breath. I can tell she's trying hard
to stay strong too. "Well, he's a great guy. A good father. We met
at the university my freshman year. He was a freshman too, and
we were in the same English class. We started dating, and we got
married right after I started working here in '71."

"What's he look like?" I realize we've never shared pictures
of family like I have with the black teachers.

"He's real good-looking. He's tall and slim and has blond
hair and blue eyes. He loves sports, all sports, but especially football, of course."

I smile. "Anthony's good-looking, tall and slim, and he
loves football too, but he's sure not blond and blue eyed."

Her chuckle warms the air between us.

"How did y'all meet?"

"We actually met at Miles College. After we married, he
and his brothers left his uncle's company and started their own
construction company. He's such a hard worker. They've built that
business up over time. I'm really proud of him." *And when I get
out of here, I'm gonna hug him tight and tell him how much I love
him, and how much I admire him. Lord, just get me out of here!*

We're quiet for a little while, probably both thinking the
same kind of thoughts about our husbands and kids, only wanting to be with them again. I guess we're alike in that way.

"Letitia," she begins, looking at me with a pleading look.
"Keep talking to me, please. When we're quiet, my mind starts
worrying, and I get more scared."

I nod. "Me too. What do you want to talk about?"

"I don't care. Anything. Tell me some more about the

Movement."

"I've told y'all the details."

"I know, but tell me something else. Tell me how y'all felt about things."

"What I felt was mad. I was angry from that time on. I guess it's taken Anthony and my little girl to get me over it."

She nods. "I can understand why you were angry."

"Yeah, but my kind of anger burned too deep, was too much. I remember how it felt, that morning of the march. We started out so hopeful, so happy. We believed we could do it, make a real difference. Then they turned the hoses on us, beat us back down so fast. Umm hmm. I remember I was wearing a locket my grandmother had given me. It was real special to me. I'd been thinking it gave me the same kind of strength and courage my Mama Lucy had, but then the water tore it off my neck and washed it away. I think it washed my courage away too. Maybe that's what made me so mad."

"Did you ever find the locket?"

I nod my head. "I kept searching until I finally did find it. I've worn it ever since. I'm wearing it now."

"I hope it holds enough courage for both of us," she says, and I see her expression showing she means those words.

"You know, I got mad during those times too. You'll think it's silly," Martha Ann says. "But it seemed like because of the blacks demonstrating and all, we couldn't have our normal life. Even though it didn't affect our neighborhood over the mountain, we couldn't do the things we might have done because our parents were afraid to let us go downtown. And we kids were afraid too, because we didn't understand. All we saw were riots and fighting on TV newscasts. We wondered if the violence would come over the mountain and hurt us."

I stay quiet. Somehow, the worries she'd had during that time don't seem so bad to me.

She looks at me. "Yeah, I know what you're thinking."

"What? What am I thinking?"

"You're thinking we were just a bunch of wimps. But look at it through our eyes. Isn't that what we have to do to finally understand each other? We have to learn each other's world. If we're ever going to get along in this one world we share now, we've got to learn each other's stories."

I feel a rising of that old anger and defensiveness, but it fizzles out as I consider the truth of what she's saying. It's not a comfortable feeling, thinking about how true her words are, but I like the idea of sharing stories. I remember that's how Yvonne and I became so close once we both started working here at Wilson. She told me all about her growing up in the Delta of Mississippi, and I told her all about growing up in the city of Birmingham. Two different worlds, but when we shared them, we knew each other, and we became friends. It seemed simple when Yvonne and I did it.

Her smile fades and is replaced by a tense, worried look. "It's gonna get dark soon, Letitia. What are we gonna do? We got to get help."

"I know. I know. If I could hear anybody nearby, we could scream, but I haven't heard a thing." I don't say that I can still hear the wind and occasional sounds of pieces of the building falling, muffled cracks and thumps that terrify me. We're under some protection, but only if something huge and heavy doesn't crash down on us. I try to push that thought out of my mind.

I feel desperate to keep us distracted. If we let ourselves get scared and panic, I don't know what could happen. "Maybe we should sing. Do you want to sing some of the old hymns?" I ask. A funny look comes over Martha Ann's face. "Not only no," she replies, "but hell no! I am the world's worst singer."

I have to smile. Singing is such a part of my life. I can't imagine not liking to sing. "Whenever my mama was upset about something, or happy about something, she would be singing. I guess we all got that from her. We could tell her mood by what she was singing. And, of course, the songs were a big part of the civil rights movement. I don't think Rev. Bevel or any of them would have gotten us up and marching if it hadn't been for the singing."

She nods. "I remember hearing 'We Shall Overcome' and thinking how powerful and moving that was."

"That wasn't the only one. Did you ever hear 'Oh, Freedom'?" I start singing, *"Oh, freedom. Oh, freedom. Oh, freedom over me, over me."*

"No, I never heard that one," she replies. "Sing some more."

"This is the chorus, *'And before I'll be a slave, I'll be buried in my grave, And go home to my Lord and be free.'* Then *'No segregation. No segregation. No segregation over me, over me.'* The other verses were *'No more weeping'* and *'No more Jim Crow'* and several others."

"Sing some more," Martha Ann urges me. I almost have to laugh, the two of us trapped here and me singing protest songs to this white person.

I start singing then, and, I swear, it takes me back to 1963, to the mass meetings, the marching. I remember how we felt then, before the hosing. We believed, God, we really believed we would make a difference. I realize how I've missed that, how my cynicism has filled my heart, instead of the hope and excitement that had been there.

I keep on singing, song after song. I belt out "We Shall Not Be Moved" and "Woke Up This Morning with My Mind Stayed on Freedom" and all those great and powerful tunes. I can see us all leaving Parker High School through the doors and the windows. Kids coming from all over Birmingham, singing, singing. I remember hearing that some came eighteen miles to join us. *What a day that was. Lord, these songs take me back.* When I get to "This Little Light of Mine," darned if Martha Ann doesn't join in. The two of us, down in this gray and scary place, singing away. It's something else. Of course, when Martha Ann sings with me, I can understand why she didn't want to sing. What a voice!

Martha Ann lies quietly for a moment after we end our duet. She looks at me, and I can see she's a little embarrassed that she tried to sing.

She sighs. "When I was in junior high, everyone was in the chorus, so, of course, I was too. But when we'd have a concert, the director would have me stand to the side, holding a cutout, like a Christmas tree at the Christmas concert. Well, this one concert, there was nothing to hold so the director told me to only mouth the words."

"Oh, Martha Ann," I say.

"That wasn't all. We were singing "Donkey Serenade," so they gave me these two sticks to hit together like the clip-clop of a donkey, you know?"

I nod.

"I couldn't even do it in rhythm, so they had to take the sticks away from me. I was throwing the whole chorus off. It was awful!"

I can tell she was remembering that as vividly as I had been recalling marching in the Movement. "Martha Ann, don't you worry about that. You can sing with me any time you want."

A look of friendly understanding and support passes between us.

5:15 p.m.

I steal a quick glance at my watch. After five o'clock. *Will the rescue searchers give up when it gets dark? Why isn't there anyone around so we can scream for help?*

"Letitia?"

"Yes?"

"Do you think, I mean, it's getting so late, do you think you should try digging your way out?"

"I've thought about that. I don't think I can do it, Martha Ann. I don't know how much has crashed down on top of us. And I worry about electrical wires and stuff."

"I know. I've thought of all that too. But how long can we

stay trapped here without food and water?"

I shrug. "It's water we need most. With all the rain that fell, you'd think there might be puddles near us, but I can't see any." I pause a moment. "I have a hard candy in my pocket that we can share, but do you think that might make us thirstier?"

"It might. Let's save that for our breakfast." Her laugh is bitter sounding.

"OK." We lie quietly. I wish I could fall asleep and wake when the rescuers come. I know we should keep talking, but I'm so tired.

I sense Martha Ann taking a deep breath, as if she's gathering her strength to her. I'm glad she is because I'm losing mine. It's slipping slowly out of my body, like the steady bleeding of a wound.

"When we get home, the first thing I'm going to eat is a cheeseburger. I'm so hungry for a cheeseburger," she says emphatically. "I can almost smell that good, greasy smell. Then, maybe, I'll have me a big slice of apple pie. Umm. Doesn't that sound good, Letitia?"

Her voice prods me from daydreams. "You're making me hungrier," I complain.

"Oh, come on, now. Let's be using our imaginations to take us out of this place. What food are you going to have, Letitia?"

I sigh, not without some exasperation. "Well, there's something I used to crave. That was an ice cream sundae with the chocolate syrup and whipped cream, and a big ole cherry on the top."

"Oh, yeah," she agrees. "Like they had at the lunch counter at Woolworth's? I remember them. Delicious."

I want to savor my memory in silence, but some part of my ornery nature stirs, and I decide to tell her why I craved those. I know it will make her uncomfortable, and, right now, I want to do that.

"But, Martha Ann, remember, we blacks couldn't go into Woolworth's and sit at the counter and order one of those delicious treats. No, that's one of the things we marched for."

She looks down. I know my words cut into her, but even so it felt good. Whites don't like to have the injustices slapped in their faces. *Oh, Lord, what's gotten into me? Why did I do that?*

Martha Ann looks back at me, and I can see a flash of defensiveness, of anger even, in her eyes. She knows I wanted to make her feel bad. And we were finally getting past all these kinds of walls between us. *Lord, Lord, help me move on. Mama Lucy, I need your strength now more than ever.*

"Once those segregation issues stopped, Letitia, did you ever go have one of those sundaes?"

I smile at her, hoping to restore something. "I sure did. One day my mama got dressed up and gathered Sam, Etta, and me, and we walked downtown, feeling proud, sitting wherever we wanted."

I let my thoughts go back to that day. It was early in the fall, the leaves of the dogwood trees were turning, though the weather was still warm. When we got to Woolworth's, we sat at the counter as big as you please. I remember the waitress. She was kind of pudgy, like she'd been eating a lot of those sundaes herself. She had that cute little apron tied 'round her, and her blonde hair was kind of in a roll under a hairnet. She took her time waiting on us, but she finally did, and I ordered one of those sundaes. When she brought our order, she slapped it down on the counter, like she'd like to dump it in our laps. I didn't care, though. I gave her a smug smile 'cause I knew she had to serve us even though she didn't want to. Mama flashed a frown at me, and I quickly dropped my expression. I dipped my spoon into that yummy concoction, being sure to get a mix of the whipped cream and chocolate along with the ice cream. Mm mm. I let it melt in my mouth, savoring every bit of it. My, oh my, it was delicious. And, somehow, I knew that the sweetness wasn't only the taste—it was being there itself.

"And was it as good as you expected?"

"Oh, yeah." I nod and smile as I remember. "Etta had a

191

sundae too, and Sam had a chocolate milk shake. I remember that Mama only ordered a cup of coffee. When I looked over at her, sipping that coffee, I thought of all that black people had gone through for such an everyday thing like having a cup of coffee. Strange, the things you remember."

Martha Ann doesn't say anything. She sinks back into herself.

Whites are so easy to read. I can tell Martha Ann is annoyed that I deliberately tried to make her feel bad. I probably should apologize, but, heck, when did a white person ever apologize to me?

The two of us lie here quietly, and I can feel our spirits sinking lower and lower. The light is beginning to fade, and so is our sense of hope. *Lord, please get us out of here. Send some rescuers soon.*

"Martha Ann, we can't let ourselves get too discouraged. We need to keep talking."

I hear her sigh real big. I hope she's putting her annoyance behind her.

"Well," she finally says, "what do you want to talk about?"

"I don't care. Do you have any more questions about the civil rights movement?" That seems to be her favorite subject.

"Even if I did, I'd hesitate to ask. Those questions only make you mad, even though I'm only asking to get more information, trying to understand your point of view." She looks at me, and I see a feistiness in her expression that I hadn't seen before. Maybe that's a good thing. It might keep us going.

"I can't help it. Anger seems like it's a part of me."

"You think every white person is a racist, don't you, Letitia? But it's really not that way."

"Oh, yeah? You think that if a person's not a member of the Klan and not burning crosses on people's lawns, they're not a racist."

"Most whites are *not* racists."

"There's all kinds of racism, Martha Ann, attitudes and actions you're probably not even aware of." *Oh, Lord, where did our friendly feelings go? We're almost snarling at each other. How did this happen?*

"So tell me about them, these other ways of showing prejudice. I really want to know."

I sigh. This is a hard subject, but it needs to see the light of day, not that there's much of that left. "OK. First off, there's active racism. You know what that is, that's what you see in blatant actions."

"Sure. I get that. That's a very small percentage of people."

"It doesn't matter how few people do it if you're the one they're doing it to," I remind her.

Her mouth forms a grim line, but she nods her understanding.

"Then there's passive racism. That's the kind we blacks see the most of."

"Oh, come on, Letitia. I know all about that idea of passive racism, so you don't need to give me any lectures."

"Are you sure you know, Martha Ann? So, tell me. What do you know about it? I'm very interested to see what you know about how black folk are treated."

"Well, I've heard that there's certain things whites do, maybe unconsciously, not even realizing it. Some white women may be driving through a black part of town, or maybe not even a black section and they see a black man, and they automatically lock their doors. I guess that's passive racism."

I look hard at her and her face colors slightly. I'm getting wound up and ready to run with this conversation so I start in. "It's like whenever there's blacks and whites in a meeting, the whites always have to be in charge."

"That's not true—" she begins, but I cut her off.

"It is true. Just by being born white, you come with a sense of entitlement or something, like there's an unwritten advantage. Whites don't see that, but I guarantee you that if you ask any black person who'll be completely honest with you, they'll tell you the truth of it."

She lies there quietly. I can tell she's thinking about it, try-ing to remember how she's acted in the past.

"How many white teachers don't expect as much from their black students, don't push them, make them work up to their potential?"

"Now, I object to that," Martha Ann responds strongly. "I'm a good teacher, and I treat all my students alike."

"And how many white or Asian or Hispanic students do you have here at Wilson?"

"None, but that isn't the point. The point is that I'm as con-scientious a teacher with every student I have. I don't see them as black or white, just kids."

"Well, now, that sounds good on the surface. But look at what you said. You don't see a black kid as black. What do you see him as, white?"

"Letitia, you're twisting my words. Have you ever seen me working with kids? No. You don't see what you don't want to see. I work hard to try to reach each and every student, no matter their race, gender, whatever, and help them be the best student they can be."

I can see that Martha Ann is really mad now, and I don't blame her. I do think she is a good teacher. "You're right," I admit. "But my point is that there are a lot of white teachers who don't expect much from the black kids, or, even worse, put them at a disadvantage. Here's what happened to my little sister, Etta, who went to an integrated school. She's really bright. Was the top speller in the whole school. But during the spelling bee to see who would represent the school at the district, it was obvi-ous the judge wanted the white boy to win. The way that judge pronounced the words so carefully for the white boy, gave him every possible advantage, slurred the words quickly for Etta, why there was no doubt the contest was stacked against her. The truth is that there really are white teachers and a lot of white employers who don't expect much from their black kids or employees. There are those glass ceilings and glass walls for blacks in the working world that whites don't even seem to see or be aware of, yet they do exist."

"But—"

"Here's another thing that happened to Etta. She was always a straight-A student. In one class, she was sitting between two good white students. When tests were handed back and all three got top grades, her teacher looked at her like she suspected her of cheating. She moved Etta's seat between the two poorest black students. When Etta continued to make top grades, the teacher was really surprised."

"Well—" she tries again, but I'm too fired up.

"Let me tell you about my cousin. He worked hard in this company, did a real good job. Gets promoted to accounts manager. He's doing fine. Then someone higher up decides they shouldn't have a black man in that job, so he gets demoted, and a completely incompetent white guy gets his position and totally screws everything up." I'm really mad now. I glare at her as I say, "Yeah. That's passive racism, and it's alive and well today."

"But, Letitia, look at how far blacks have come since the '60s. That black lawyer—I forget his name—got on city council a few years ago, and now that other black guy is on it. There's lots of black business executives in Birmingham."

I smile. I know my history. "That black lawyer is Arthur Shores, and Richard Arrington is a councilman now. Sure, but the population of Birmingham is at least what—45 percent blacks? Until the late '60s there wasn't a single black in city government. Having a token black only means one vote on the council for almost half the city's population."

"Be fair, Letitia, things are getting more equal all the time."

Now, it's my turn to back down a little, because she's right.

"Speaking of attitudes, as a white person in Birmingham, and in this school, I certainly have felt that blacks don't want to try and be friends. They hold us at arm's length."

I have no comment on that because I know it's true.

TURNER

"And what about affirmative action?" she asks. "Hasn't that helped a lot?"

"That's a good question. Sometimes it's helped and sometimes it's hurt."

"What do you mean?"

"Well, it's helped because it was necessary to start fairer hiring practices. Without affirmative action, a lot of companies and the government wouldn't have given blacks a chance. But the idea of affirmative action was to stop discrimination in hiring and also to hire the most qualified person even if he or she came from a minority race, right?"

She nods. "Yes."

"But sometimes, things got turned 'round. Fearing lawsuits, some employers simply hired any black, even unqualified ones, setting them up for failure and reinforcing the whites' idea that blacks haven't got what it takes to succeed."

Martha Ann remains quiet as she's considering what I have said.

I continue. "When whites see incompetent blacks hired over them, what do you think that does for racial attitudes? And when blacks see incompetent whites hired over *them*, the same kind of feelings happen."

"I can see that," she acknowledges.

"I read about a study they did, 'cause I care about this. They studied all these blacks that got into college in spite of their grades or SAT scores, in other words, through affirmative action. Of those, more than half went on and got advanced degrees, and almost half got PhDs, or became doctors or lawyers, percentages much higher than for regular college students. These are folks who wouldn't have had more than a high-school education if it weren't for affirmative action."

She shakes her head. "I feel like you're trying to give me a course on 'Race Relations 101.' You think whites are completely unaware? That we know nothing about it? How about you, Letitia? Do you know anything about how life is for me?"

196

I want to answer back with anger when her words hit me. Have I ever tried to see things from a white's viewpoint? We both fall silent.

5:50 p.m.

We stay quiet for a while. I imagine we're both thinking about the words we hurled at each other, maybe wishing we hadn't sounded so angry, and I bet we're both praying for someone to come soon.

Martha Ann clears her throat. "What I wouldn't give for something to drink."

"Me too, but it's probably better not to be thinking about that."

She gives a little rueful laugh. "Do we dare keep talking, though? We might get ourselves into a real fight."

I have an embarrassed smile on my face. "Yeah."

Her expression becomes serious again. "But you know, Letitia, maybe that's a good thing. I mean, there is anger and misunderstanding on both sides. Maybe the reason we as whites and blacks can't mix better is because we don't acknowledge that anger."

I think about her words. "Maybe so. I know when Anthony and I are mad about something, until we get it out in the open, we don't get it resolved."

"Exactly. But how in the world do we do that? And would bringing out that anger cause things like demonstrations and riots, and what good would that do?"

I shake my head. "I don't know. I'd hate to think we had to trap a white and a black together in every tornado to get them to finally talk honestly to each other."

We both smile. Silence sifts around us like the settling of the dust, but now it's a comfortable silence as we each consider our own thoughts.

Martha Ann gives a choked, almost bitter-sounding laugh.

TURNER

"Look at the two of us. We've worked together for years. We've never had an argument or a cross word, or any reason to ever mistrust one another, have we?"

I have to agree. "No, we haven't."

"And yet, we've never really talked to each other. We've never shared in any personal way. Is it that way all across the South, maybe the whole country? Now that we're integrated, do we still keep the very essence of ourselves segregated?"

I think about her words. She's right. Even Mae, teaching now in what had been an all-white school, going to a Bible study with a mixed-race group at the Episcopal church. Does Mae have any white friends she is as close to as her black friends? I don't think so.

I answer, "Well, we're still segregated in so many ways. How many neighborhoods are really integrated? We're still seeing so much white flight farther out into Vestavia, Mountain Brook, and all those areas outside the city. Seems like our Birmingham city schools are becoming blacker and blacker. How many churches are integrated? How many women's clubs? How many golf courses?"

Martha Ann nods her agreement. "That's true. But is it because we can't mix in those areas, or is it that we don't want to?"

"By we, do you mean you whites?" I hear a sneer in my voice, my old anger stirring up.

"No! By we I mean us, us as Southerners, as Americans, as people."

"OK. I'll accept that we means all of us. And, I think the truth is that we—whites and blacks—don't really want to mix."

We're quiet for a while. I can see Martha Ann nod slowly.

"But," she begins. "But are we afraid to mix because we don't really know each other? If we did mix more comfortably, wouldn't we find good relationships with each other that enriched both of us?"

"Maybe." I reluctantly have to agree.

Martha Ann looks straight ahead, seeming to be looking

deep into her heart. "I want to tell you a little something about me, about when I was a teenager." She pauses as I shift into a more comfortable position, if there is such a thing.

"I want to share this with you so that maybe you'll see how things were from my perspective, OK?"

"Sure," I agree, although I have never considered a white person's perspective before. I'm not sure I want to.

"I told you that my dad was a racist. When I started high school that was right when the demonstrations were starting, the Children's March, all of that. Now, try to remember being a high-school girl. What was the most important thing on a high-school girl's mind?"

That's easy. "Boys. Being accepted. Being part of the group."

"Exactly. And, Letitia, I can assure you that there wasn't a single group of teenagers in any white school in the South that was going around saying, 'Let's integrate. Let's become friends with black kids.' Why? Because we had never been around blacks. All we knew about blacks was what we had been taught by our parents, who had been taught by their parents. We believed things about blacks because we didn't know any better. We were taught all those negative things, like blacks were less intelligent, were dirtier, wanted to fight, and we didn't have any life experience with them to see anything differently. And the only thing we'd seen about black kids our age was their protesting, was the riots."

"Yes, but—"

"Wait, let me finish. Back then, in high school, I began to understand how unfair things were for blacks in the South, and I wanted things to be made right. Yet, there was no way for me, as an individual, to make any difference. If I spoke up at home, my dad became angry and wanted to punish me. If I had spoken up at school to my friends, they wouldn't want anything to do with me. Do you see?"

I don't say anything.

"I did have one friend, Connie," Martha Ann says, thinking

back to those years. "She didn't care what other people thought of her. She'd make comments supporting blacks, even though many in our class shunned her. She didn't care even though she didn't really know any blacks, didn't participate in any of the demonstrations. But most people wouldn't have spoken up like that, especially in high school. We had to feel like we belonged, were part of the group." She pauses, remembering Connie. "After college, she moved to California. We've lost touch, but I bet she fit in very well out there."

After a moment of silence, Martha Ann picks up the thread of our conversation. "Not only was support for blacks an unacceptable view, but because of the blacks, things in my world were falling apart. When it finally became time when they had to integrate the schools, they brought in four black boys into our school. When my dad drove us to the Christmas Dance that year, he saw the four black guys and their dates going into the dance, and he wouldn't let me go in. I couldn't go to the most important dance of the year because of blacks. Do you think that made me feel supportive of them?"

Martha Ann goes on, as if imploring me to understand. "So I didn't speak out for blacks. What good would it have done? I was one voice, one girl who didn't really understand what it was all about."

When I look at her again, she's weeping.

She turns toward me, not even trying to wipe away her tears. "And so, I said nothing. I did nothing to change things. I went along on the tide of feelings that flowed around me. I just went along. It seemed like that was all I could do. I didn't even try."

I'm quiet. I don't know what to say. I don't like admitting it, but I can understand how it was for her. That doesn't make it right. That doesn't change how things were, how they are now. But I almost can hear Mama Lucy whispering in my ear, saying *"but, sugar, that can change how things will be."* And I want to believe my grandmother. For the first time since that May morning when I marched out of the Sixteenth Street Baptist Church,

I want to believe again. I remember that feeling of hope, and my eyes fill with tears.

Martha Ann looks at me and continues, "Letitia, I want to say, I need to say, I'm sorry. I'm sorry for the way blacks were treated, and I'm sorry that I wasn't strong enough to do something." She stretches her arm toward me, her hand opening for mine.

My throat has a catch in it. I couldn't speak even if I had the words. Here in the graying light, trapped under beams and debris, I lean in her direction and I take her hand in mine. I look at our hands together, white and black, and for this brief moment in time, I find that I truly can believe in reconciliation. Maybe, I've learned a valuable lesson, that this is the way it starts, one by one, sharing honestly. And as anger about the past dims, and hope for the future remains vague, I celebrate this moment. This precious, special moment.

I'm not sure of my voice, so I simply nod toward Martha Ann. We each squeeze hands, and let go, shifting back a little. Neither of us seems to want to break the moment with words, so we lie quietly.

CHAPTER TWENTY

Reconciliation: *To make oneself or another no longer opposed. To make two apparently conflicting things compatible or consistent with each other.*

6:30 p.m.

It's getting dark, and I close my eyes. Maybe I doze off, I'm not sure. Suddenly, I'm jolted into awareness. Beams of light are swinging 'round us. Martha Ann and I look at each other with excitement, and we both start screaming, "Help!" and "We're here!" and "Save us!"

I hear voices, many voices, and lights are swirling all over. My heart is racing so fast, and I'm trembling all over. I want to push everything off me and run toward the voices.

Finally, there is one voice, a man's. "Keep talking so we can tell exactly where you are."

"We're here," I say, not knowing what else to say. "We're under what was a big table in the teachers' lounge." That seems like a silly thing to say 'cause, of course, there is no more teachers' lounge.

"Keep talking," he urges us. There's more light now. I can't believe how good the sound of his voice makes me feel.

I look at Martha Ann, and she starts talking. "We're close together, but there's a beam or something trapping my leg. Can you tell where we are yet?"

"We're very near," says this wonderful, strong voice. "There's a lot of stuff down in this area, so we've got to be real careful. We're almost there, don't y'all worry. We'll get you out."

"Thank you! Thank God!" we both respond. We look at each other and smile. I keep talking. "There's two of us here, Martha Ann Reynolds and Letitia Williams. There were two other teachers still here at school. Have you found them? Are they trapped too?"

"I don't know," the man answered. "But don't worry. We've got rescuers combing this whole area. If they're here, we'll get them out."

I hear the sounds of things being moved, like chunks of cement and beams of wood. I hear lots of voices more softly in the background. I feel a tingling all over, like I want to burst out of my skin, I want to get out of here so badly.

The good voice continues, "Are either of you hurt, any bleeding, broken bones?"

"We're OK," I say, "except Martha Ann's leg is trapped. Once all this stuff is off me, I can move and get out."

"That's good. That's all very good," he answers. "We'll work toward one of you at a time, but don't worry. We're going to get you both out. Which one has the trapped leg?"

"It's me, Martha Ann," she responds. "I'm very close to Letitia, but a little to her side."

"OK. I've got your location pinpointed. Now, y'all just hang on a little while, and we'll safely get all this stuff on top of you moved away. Don't you worry about a thing."

I love this man, his strong voice. I want to give him a hug as soon as I get out of here. The sounds of digging and tossing stuff go on. The light gets brighter as it filters through what's still over us.

Suddenly, a shout, a warning! *Oh, my God, what's happening?* There's a roar as things shake and move around us. We both are screaming. Martha Ann's glance catches mine, and I know her expression of terror mirrors my own. *Are we gonna die?*

"Hang on! Hang on!" the strong voice shouts at us. Lights flicker. Are they leaving?

"Don't go! Please, don't go!" I can't help shouting.

His voice comes back. "Now, take it easy. There's no way we would leave y'all, I promise. Things have shifted a little out here, that's all. It happens sometimes, but we'll still get both of you out. Did any more of the debris come on top of you in there? Did that change things for you?"

I look at Martha Ann, and she shakes her head. There's a fine powder of dust that stirred up, so it's harder to see each other. "No," I answer.

It's so hard to lie here and not try to jump up and run to the rescuers. I feel like I'm holding my breath, and Martha Ann seems to be too. Instead of only minutes, it is like hours since we first heard their voices. I hear the strong voice shouting back to someone. He says our names. I hear the scraping and working with the collapsed building, and I try to picture them getting closer and closer.

The man calls in to us. "We've got a couple a' very anxious husbands out here. Y'all interested in seeing anyone named Bill or Anthony?" He chuckles.

Martha Ann and I look at each other with joy overflowing our faces. "Yes," we both cry at once. Simply knowing our husbands are there waiting for us makes us feel wonderful, like we're almost in their arms and safe—safe again. Safe! It's the first I've let myself think that word. Just thinking the word "safe" makes me feel Anthony's strong embrace. *Oh, God, make them hurry!*

Light shines brighter around Martha Ann, like she's on stage in the spotlight. She tries to turn so she can look up, but with her leg caught, she can't do it.

Then, it happens. I can see a man sliding sideways beyond her, working his way toward the wooden trap over her leg.

"Howdy," he says and smiles. "I'm Roger." He's wearing a hard hat and some special vest with glowing strips of fabric. The rest of his clothes are covered with dust and mud.

We both nod at him, but neither one of us can say a word. I'm sure Martha Ann's heart is racing as fast as mine. We can't take our gaze off this rescuer. He looks us over quickly and says,

TURNER

"Well, y'all are looking mighty good for being trapped here like this."

He scoots down to the beam of wood holding Martha Ann prisoner. The light attached to his hard hat sends rays up and down the length of it, and then he eases back to the opening behind him.

He pats Martha Ann's shoulder. "Now, little lady, we'll have you out of here soon. Give us a few minutes to get everything set up, OK?"

"OK," she says and her voice is as shaky as I feel.

As he disappears into the blackness I feel a rush of panic. I suddenly can hardly breathe; my chest hurts as I gasp for breath. Martha Ann's expression is full of terror.

His voice makes its way back to us. "I'm right here. I'm not going anywhere." He must have known our reaction even though he couldn't see us. "I've got to have them bring me some equipment. We need to prop up that wood to get your leg out. It won't take long."

We both sigh deeply, trying to get our balance again. We look at each other, and this time I reach out my hand to hers. We lock hands and squeeze hard before we let go. We don't need words anymore. We are together in this.

Soon he's back with what looks like the jack for a car. He slides it under the beam on one side of her leg. He backs out again and quickly returns with another jack for the other side of her leg. "Now I want you to lie still, absolutely still. Can you do that?"

Martha Ann nods. Her expression reminds me of my little girl before she jumped in the pool for the first time.

"When this old piece of wood lifts off your leg, you're gonna want to pull your leg away. Don't do that. Hear me, now? Just lie still, and I'm going to pull you out. Got it?"

"I'll lie still. I promise."

He chuckles again, a warm, deep sound that helps us relax a little.

206

He lies flat and jacks up one side an inch. He shifts around and jacks up the other side the same amount. Looking back at Martha Ann he says, "Doing OK?"

Her voice is a whisper. "Yes."

He jacks up the first side a fraction more. For the first time I can see light between Martha Ann's leg and the beam of wood. As he reaches for the second jack, suddenly everything shifts toward me, I feel what was the tabletop slam against me. For a second I can't see anything. I'm screaming, screaming, but my chest hurts so much I don't have any breath. My screams are like silent ghosts, full of nothingness. I hear Martha Ann yell my name. The man shouts words to the others, or maybe to me; I can't understand. What's happening? After all this, am I gonna die? Anthony's so close outside. Will I ever see him again? My heart is hammering so loudly, I can't hear anything else.

Everything starts to settle—dust, lights, sounds. I shake my head to clear my thoughts. I can hear that man, Roger, talking to me now.

"You're OK, don't be afraid. We'll get you out. Everything's OK."

All soothing words, but somehow, they don't calm me. I feel the pressure of wood lying on top of me. *Lord, God, please, please!* Those are the only words I can pray. I've never been so scared.

Roger keeps talking. "I'm going to pull Martha Ann out now, then I'm going to get you out. Understand? I'll get you next. You've got nothing to worry about. We're all here to get you safely out of this mess. Honest."

I look at him and my face is full of fear. I can't help it. What if everything collapses on top of me before he gets back to me? I've got to stay alive for Felicia, for Anthony.

My glance sweeps over to Martha Ann. She's looking at me like she wants to say something, like she doesn't want to leave me alone in here. *Alone? Oh, God, I'm going to be alone. Don't leave me alone!* I want to scream, to cry out to take me too.

TURNER

Roger is backing out, his hands firmly pulling Martha Ann with him. Her hand stretches toward me, but she's out of my reach now. Her gaze holds mine, like she's sending me some message, what? Without words between us, I feel her telling me to be strong, that she's sorry to leave me alone. I feel her caring deeply about what happens to me, and that makes a difference. Somehow that makes a difference, and I do feel stronger. I put my hand to my locket. At least I can still do that.

I take deep breaths, even though it hurts. There's cheering outside, and I realize that Martha Ann is safe. I'm next! I know I'll be out there soon. I will!

The next half hour is a blur. Roger comes back and forth, bringing equipment, braces, I don't know what all. The whole time he talks to me, tries to calm me, jokes about Anthony. Everything's a crazy swirl of lights and noise, people shouting back and forth, things being moved over us. And then, there's that moment—Oh, Lord, what a moment! Roger helps me scoot myself free. Free! I'm out in the open again. There's air to breathe; there's nothing over me but the night sky! *Thank you, Lord! Thank you, my Jesus.*

They lift me onto a stretcher, and suddenly Anthony is there, his hand holding mine, kissing me.

"Letitia, I love you, girl. I love you."

I laugh, the joy comes bubbling out, and I laugh and cry at the same time. "Felicia? Is she all right?" My chest hurts, but it doesn't matter now.

Anthony nods firmly. "She's with your mama. She's fine."

They push my stretcher over to the ambulance, and the paramedics are asking me questions, checking me over.

"Where's Roger?" I ask. "I want to thank Roger, give him a hug."

Everyone 'round me is smiling, and someone calls Roger over.

I take his hand and look up into his kind face. "How can I ever thank you?"

He shakes his head. "Just keep on being a good teacher," he says. "I'm glad you and Martha Ann are OK." He turns away, and Anthony is right back by my side.

"They're going to take you and Martha Ann to the hospital to check you out and be real sure you're OK," says Anthony.

"Did they find Yvonne and Mr. Mills?" I ask. "Are they OK?"

"I'll find out, honey. Let me go see." He walks away, and I want to yell for him to come back. I need him by my side. But then I'm ashamed of such a selfish thought. I do want to know about the others.

Anthony returns quickly, smiling to reassure me. "They've got them, and they're on the way to the hospital too. They had been going to their cars when they saw the tornado almost here, and they ran back to the school. Evidently, they got there in the nick of time and were in the hallway. The rescuers got to them about an hour ago."

I look over and see Martha Ann still here on a stretcher a few feet away, her tall, blond husband by her side. She's looking at me and smiling real big.

Anthony nods in her direction. "She wouldn't let them take her to the hospital till she knew you were safely out of there."

I try to smile, but it feels more like a grimace. I can't say a word for the lump in my throat. Tears are pooling in my eyes, so everything looks kind of blurry. With all the lights they've put up around us and the tears in my eyes, everything sparkles, bright, and beautiful. I like this view of the world. There's a humming of good feelings through me, and I believe it's the coming back of hope, hope for a better tomorrow. Will Martha Ann and I become best friends forever? Probably not. But now we will be friends. Like my Mama Lucy seemed to whisper in my ear, things can change in the future. People can reconcile and make a better tomorrow for all of us. We will have to work at it but we *can* work at it. That's the important thing.

I put my hand to my throat. I can feel the weight of the

locket there, reminding me, reaffirming all the good lessons
Mama Lucy tried to teach me, the sense of hope she tried to leave
with me.

As they lift me into the ambulance, I lift my hand in a slight
wave to Martha Ann, and she does the same back to me.

~

History—days of giving and taking, laughing and crying, dreaming and doing—continued. Eventually the children of the March
became adults.

And there was hope.

DISCUSSION QUESTIONS

1. How was it possible for Martha Ann to remain so naïve about life for blacks in the community?

2. Why do you think Letitia held on to so much anger against whites as an adult?

3. What do you think about the way black children were protected from knowing how much discrimination was around them?

4. Why do you think the relationship between Mama Lucy and Letitia was so strong?

5. How do you imagine the relationship between Letitia and Martha Ann continued over time?

6. How do our attitudes toward race develop? How do you think Letitia's and Martha Ann's attitudes developed?

7. What role do you think television had in making the civil rights movement a national issue?

8. Given Dr. King's reluctance to use the children in the protests, do you think this was the right thing to do?

9. The children who participated in the Children's March were naïve about the consequences of their action, but, clearly, they were committed. What was it that gave them this commitment?

10. Do you think it's helpful or hurtful to acknowledge the atrocities of whites against blacks in our history?

11. Do you think these historical events are documented in our history?

12. What do you think might be an effective process for reconciliation? What can an individual do toward racial and ethnic understanding and reconciliation?

Rosalie T. Turner has been writing for nearly 30 years. Her historical novel, *Sisters of Valor*, won a Military Writers Society of America Award for Fiction and was selected by the Army Wife Network book club.

Her third book, *Freedom Bound*, received a top award from Florida First Coast Writers. In 1998 she was awarded the JC Penney Award for establishing an inner city reading program in Florida.

Rosalie is a graduate of Mary Washington College. Before writing full-time, she worked as a juvenile probation officer and as a Director of Christian Education. She and her husband divide their time between Alabama and New Mexico.

FREEDOM BOUND
ISBN# 978-0-9679483-3-1

SISTERS OF VALOR
ISBN# 978-0-9792375-2-2

BEYOND THE DREAM
ISBN# 145378747X

GOING TO THE MOUNTAIN
ISBN# 1-4141-0686-6

MY VERY OWN BOOK OF THE LORD'S PRAYER
ISBN# 0-687-27554-7

Follow Rosalie Turner on her website – www.rosalieturner.com – or her blog – http://blog.rosalieturner.com.

CPSIA information can be obtained
at www.ICGtesting.com
Printed in the USA
FFOW03n0120110218
44943618-45191FF